REGINA RODGERS AND LYN LANDAU

DANGER ON THE NAVAJO NATION

By
Regina Rodger and Lyn Landau

Editor: Cynthia Hickey
Book Design by Winged Publications

ISBN-13:978-1-968792-26-8

Acknowledgements:

Thank you to the amazing writers who assist and inspire us. Without groups like Mid-America Romance Authors (MARA) or American Christian Fiction Writers (ACFW), this book might never have been written.

Other Books by Regina Rodgers:

Winding Roads to Love series:
The Gamble on Love
The Long Road to Love

Stay up to date with us on ReginaRodgers.com and LynLandau.com!

Chapter One

Maggie Beaumont parked in front of the sad, brownish mobile home and stared at it over the top of her sunglasses. It looked small, surrounded by desert, sunbaked in the scant shade of a mesquite tree. A shiver ran down her spine.

She pasted on a smile. "So… this is it."

Terri kicked her feet off the Jeep's dashboard, taking it in. "Your surprise inheritance?"

"This plus a lease on twenty acres—courtesy of a father I never met."

They sat in silence a moment, the wind teasing grit through the air. Dark clouds brooded over the burnished Lukachukai Mountains, threatening a downpour.

"Well." Maggie shut off the engine. "Let's see what the mystery man left behind."

Terri hesitated. "You sure this is the right place?"

"If it's not, somebody's about to get two very confused visitors."

The small wooden stoop groaned under Maggie's weight. She fumbled with the key, but the door creaked open before she touched the lock.

"It's already open?" Terri reached around Maggie and pushed on it.

The door moaned open, a slow, reluctant sound. For a moment, she thought she heard something shift in the shadows beyond.

"Why is it unlocked?"

Maggie crept into the small, dusty living room. She stood still and scanned the vestiges of what had been her father's home—a father she'd never laid eyes on, whose voice she'd never heard.

"I don't know." Her friend's pale eyes were wide, and she swallowed with a click. "But it's about to pour, so let's take the grand tour." She put a hand on Maggie's shoulder and steered her into the small mobile home.

Faux wood-paneled walls surrounded the shaded figures of a built-in sofa with an old blanket thrown over it. In the corner, an aged writing desk stood vigil. Glancing under it, two small bowls caught her eye. She stopped in her tracks. "He had a pet. I wonder what happened to it?"

They moved through the kitchen with its peeling turquoise paint. Maggie flipped the light switch, and it clicked uselessly.

"I can see the clock on the stove. The electricity's connected, so why aren't the lights working?" A surge of gooseflesh climbed Maggie's arms, and she chafed her hands up and down them.

Terri's laugh was weak. "Maybe the bulbs burnt out?"

"Yeah… maybe."

Terri scoffed again. "Mr. Maggie's Dad, you were not much of a housekeeper." She ran a finger across the chipped laminate countertop. "How can this much dust accumulate in a few weeks?"

"Are you kidding? Every time someone drives down this road, a cloud of dust flies everywhere." Maggie turned to look out the window when something out of place grabbed her attention. A plastic grocery bag sat tucked into the corner of the counter. A six-pack of soda peeked out of the bag, condensation shining on the bottles.

Maggie's heart lurched. She turned silently to Terri and grasped her arm. "Look." She whispered and pointed to the sodas. "Those things are still cold. Somebody's just been here."

Something crashed behind the mobile home. Terri jumped and let out a shriek. "What was that?"

Maggie turned to the back door. "Maybe my dad's long-lost pet."

"Or maybe it's a bobcat."

"Okay, I think my imagination is running away with me. Probably, the lawyer was here before us and left in a hurry. We should finish doing what we came here for." Maggie lifted the curtain over the door and peeked outside. "Let's go take a look at the back deck."

The metal door creaked open onto a small, covered porch. A lump tightened Maggie's throat. "Almost like he was sitting here having coffee this morning."

She trailed her fingers through a thin line of dust on the back of an old lawn chair, eyeing the empty coffee mug on the rickety side table.

As she gazed off to the northeast, the vista before her took her breath away. *No wonder he'd wanted to live here.* Three flat-topped sandstone mesas loomed before her, the red rock now shrouded in inky storm clouds.

"Amazing, isn't it?" Terri twisted her blonde hair into a bun and adjusted her ball cap over it. She gazed at the view.

"Yeah. Amazing is the word."

A gust of cool wind blew across them, carrying the scent of wet sage and juniper. This storm would break soon.

"We'd better finish looking around. That rain's gonna reach us any minute now. I'll go see what's in this little building out here. Hopefully, I don't find a bobcat in the shed. You should finish inspecting the inside." Terri stepped off the porch and sprinted across the backyard.

Maggie headed inside the shadowy mobile home, passed through the kitchen, and made her way to the bedroom. At the doorway, she paused, hesitant to enter her father's private, personal space. She took tentative steps into the room, the noise too loud in the oppressive silence.

She opened the closet door to see faded shirts, half falling off their hangers, and a pair of western boots amid a few other shoes on the floor. On the shelf, she noticed a small cardboard box. She lifted it down and read the words written with permanent marker across the top. *Photos, letters, misc.*

Photos? Maybe I'll get to see what he looked like.

She opened the box. Resting on top was a picture of a handsome Navajo man with his arm around a young, fair-skinned woman. She flipped it over and read the back. *Me and Jackie, August, 1998.*

Her mother had claimed her real dad was a man from back east, who'd died when she was a baby. Mom had always shut down any effort to ask questions about her father. *Mom, imagine how it feels to learn you're half Navajo at twenty-five.*

Thunder rumbled, interrupting her thoughts, and raindrops thumped on the roof. Maggie snatched up the box and hurried to the back door. "Terri, let's head back to camp! And I've got something to show you. You won't believe what I found in the closet."

No answer.

"I said, let's go!"

Her stomach sank. She set the box on the kitchen table and ran out the door. "Terri, come on." Her voice rose in volume and pitch. "The rain will be torrential any minute now."

Maggie bounded toward the work shed, the scent of wet earth thickening around her as the storm closed in.

She shouted to Terri again, her mind spinning. Maybe Terri simply couldn't hear her calling over the noise of the storm. Maybe she was already back at the Jeep. Raindrops pelted her shoulders like gravel and stung her skin. She dashed across the muddy yard, seeking protection under the shelter of the shed's roof.

"Terri?" She called out. "I said we need to get going."

No reply. The silence from the shed was worse than any sound. Not a creak. Not even a breath.

Maggie touched the door handle and leaned against it. The hair on the back of her neck lifted. Her instincts screamed at her to turn back. A sudden intuition told her something was very wrong. She shook her head to clear it.

With a firm grip, she pulled the shed door open

and peered inside. The gray sky and lack of windows left the interior shrouded in shadow. With a few cautious steps, she entered the room, straining her eyes in the sparse light.

Before her vision could adjust to the dimness of the building, footsteps shuffled behind her. A pair of strong hands grabbed both her shoulders and whirled her around.

A flash of motion—a figure—then pain exploded across her jaw.

Her legs gave out. The floor rushed up.

Thunder cracked in her skull. And then—darkness.

In a corner of her mind, she heard Terri scream.

Her head pounding, Maggie raised up onto her elbows, uncertain what had just happened or how much time had passed. The storm lashed the shed with a fury now. She reached for one of the shelves that lined the wall and pulled herself to her feet.

Every shadow looked like it might move. The walls closed in.

What if he's still here?

She forced her limbs to move, her heart thudding in her throat. She took a shaky breath. Her thoughts raced toward her friend.

"Terri?" She barely dared breathe the word. She stumbled across the floor, her gaze finally landing on the motionless figure in the corner. Terri lay crumpled on the ground, still as death.

Maggie hurried to her side, flipped the young woman onto her back, and patted her face. "Terri!" She moved her hand away and found blood on her fingers. With trembling hands, she pulled her cell phone from her jeans pocket and dialed 911.

~

Wind whistled through the cracked-open windows of Navajo Tribal Police Officer Nathan Yazzie's cruiser. Switching on the windshield wipers, his knuckles blanched against the steering wheel as rain pelted the slick, oily road. The dotted lines marking the two lanes blurred beneath the pouring rain.

Johnny Cash's voice crackled and then faded to static as he drove through the rocky pass, returning from Lukachukai. Nathan sighed and switched to another station. The music went silent as the police radio picked up and the clipped voice of Officer Sarah Nez filtered through. "Sergeant Yazzie?"

He snatched up the radio mic. "Go ahead, dispatch."

"We got an emergency call. A 10-24. A *bilagaàna* woman injured on the Adakai property off Route 7."

Nathan nodded. "En route."

Officer Nez paused a moment, letting the line pop with static before she spoke again. "By the way, the lieutenant says your rookie will start today. He'll meet you on site."

Nathan blew out a frustrated breath. At twenty-seven, he was young but had been on the job for a few years. So far, he'd avoided the dreaded job of training a rookie. He frowned. "10-4, dispatch."

There was another pause, then the music came back in. Nathan heaved a deep sigh. Okay, if Lieutenant

Benjamin Benally, Uncle Ben to Nathan, wanted him to train a rookie, he guessed he'd have to do it.

In ten minutes, he arrived at the Adakai place and grabbed his poncho from the backseat. He jumped out of the car, rain speckling his shoulders as thunder rumbled around him.

A young woman rushed from a utility shed behind the mobile home, wet, long, dark hair clinging to her face and neck.

"I'm so glad you're here." She squinted up at him through thick eyelashes bunched over nearly black eyes.

"You reported an assault?"

She nodded, and he followed her back to the outbuilding. "Yes, she's in here. Terri Mitchell. We're both adjunct professors for the Department of Anthropology at UNM, Albuquerque. We're on the dig at Canyon de Chelly and drove out here to–" She shook her head. "Sorry. You don't want to hear all this."

"It's fine, Ms...."

"Maggie. Margaret Beaumont. I just inherited this place from my dad, John Adakai."

Nathan nodded. *I recognize that name. He was Mom's friend and neighbor.*

"Take a deep breath, Ms. Beaumont. We'll get there. Emergency services are on the way, and I'm here to ensure everyone is safe." He reached up and pulled a string that hung from a light fixture in the ceiling. Light bloomed in the small space.

Maggie pinched her eyes closed and seconds later, looked at him again. She rubbed her jaw, then gestured to the far end of the work shed. "I've got her settled over there. I think the bleeding has slowed. She's... scrambled, though."

Nathan nodded and walked past Maggie. Terri lay on the floor, tacky blood staining her blonde hair and pooling beside her. Head wounds bled a lot, though. It might not be as bad as it looked, but he'd leave that to the experts. Her blue eyes settled on him as he crouched in front of her.

"Ma'am, I'm Officer Nathan Yazzie. What happen to you? How did you hurt your head?"

Terri tried to sit up, flinched, and Nathan laid a hand on her shoulder. "No, stay put. Paramedics will be here soon."

Terri rubbed her forehead, confusion in her eyes. "I'm not sure what happened. I was looking around in here and out of nowhere, it felt like somebody tried to use my head for softball practice. Next thing I knew, Maggie was standing over me, waking me up."

"So, someone hit you? Did you see the person who did it?"

"No." She shook her head, then she winced and stopped short. "I didn't see anyone. They must have come up behind me." She cringed in pain.

Behind him, Maggie spoke up. "I saw a tall, slender man, dressed all in black. He came up behind me, whirled me around, punched me, and knocked me to the ground. Then he must have hit Terri."

The purple bruise darkened even as he spoke to her. Nathan's blood boiled. "Yeah, I see you're injured. We'll need to have the paramedics check you out, too. Both of you, sit tight." He stood, pulled a flashlight from his duty belt, and began a quick inspection of the shed. Metal shelves, a box of broken pottery, and a bunch of rusted tools.

Maggie sat down next to Terri, cross-legged, and held a tissue to Terri's head.

A timid voice spoke from the doorway. "Excuse me, ma'am, but maybe you should wait for paramedics to take care of that."

Every eye turned toward the door.

A short, skinny, uniformed man in his early twenties looked at Nathan. "Mervin Yoyetewa. I'm your new recruit." His lopsided smile dissolved at the stern look he received from his new training officer. He looked up at the significantly taller Nathan and extended his hand.

Nathan paused, then shook it. He holstered his flashlight and crossed his arms. "Yoyetewa? That sounds like a Hopi name?"

"Yes, sir. My dad is Hopi."

Vehicle engines and the squishing of tires through mud put an end to their conversation. Emergency services pulled up in front of the mobile home and EMTs hustled into the outbuilding.

As paramedics began their examination, Nathan led Maggie and Yoyetewa outside. Rain drummed down against the metal roof of the shed.

Officer Yoyetewa laughed. "Isn't this a great way to start a partnership?"

Maggie scurried into the mobile home, but Nathan stopped his rookie at the door. "We're not partners, Yoyetewa. I am your training officer and you've got a long way to go to prove yourself."

The other man wilted. His voice went quiet. "Yes, sir."

"I'm going inside so I can finish my report. I want you to stay close to Ms. Mitchell. Let us know when the paramedics have finished their assessment." Nathan stepped into the mobile home and the screen door snapped closed behind him.

He pulled off his dripping wet poncho and hung it over the top of the back door, pulled a pad and pen from his pants pocket, and sat down opposite Maggie.

Drenched and shivering, she sat with her arms crossed. As she stared up at him with her wide, dark eyes, a wave of protectiveness washed over him, leaving him strangely compelled to keep her safe.

"Miss Beaumont. Would you like to take a few minutes to change clothes and dry your hair?"

She shivered and shook her head no. "This is my late father's mobile home. I don't live here. This is actually the first time I've been inside this place—first time I've been to this reservation at all—so I don't have any belongings here."

He couldn't bear watching as she sat there, soaking wet and trembling. "You're gonna catch cold, Miss Beaumont. Let me get you my jacket from the cruiser." He grabbed his poncho and raced out the front door. Returning a moment later, he handed her his brown, quilted jacket. She gratefully wrapped it around her shoulders and shivered again.

"Thank you, Officer... I'm sorry, what was it?"

"Yazzie. Nathan Yazzie."

"Thank you, Officer Yazzie."

"You're welcome." He sat down at the table and opened his notepad. "Okay, can you start from the beginning? What happened today?"

She took a deep breath. "Well, Terri and I are both working on a new dig at Canyon de Chelly. We're camped there with our team. Our supervisor is Professor Bruce Adams.

"My father, John Adakai, just passed away a couple of weeks ago. I inherited this mobile home, and Terri and I came out today to look things over. Terri went out to the shed to look around in there. When I called her to come inside, there was no response, so I went to check on her. Some man in a black hoodie came out of the corner and hit me, then I guess he hit Terri."

"Can you describe him?"

Maggie frowned. "Unfortunately, it happened so fast, and it was so dark in the shed, I didn't really get a good look at him. I'm sorry, all I can tell you is he was a little taller than me and with an average build."

Nathan looked up from his notepad. She held her hand to her jaw, barely able to open her mouth now. He shook his head. "You need some ice on that." He went to the fridge and bundled some ice cubes in a towel. "Here. Hold that up to your jaw."

"Thank you." She placed the cold pack to her face and shivered again.

Nathan sat down at the table and refocused his attention on the wet and injured young woman across from him. He tapped his pen on the notepad before him. "Miss Beaumont, did anyone else know about you inheriting this property?"

"No, just Terri and, of course, the probate attorney who contacted me. I haven't even told my mother yet." She looked away and shook her head. "It's complicated."

"What is that attorney's name?"

"Jefferson. I think it was Donald Jefferson, in Albuquerque—my hometown."

Nathan made a note, then looked up. "I'll check a few things out, but I think this was probably some petty thief who knew nobody's living here right now. He was probably looking to pilfer something to pawn for a few dollars. You and Miss Mitchell came in at the wrong time and he panicked." *Otherwise, you'd both be dead.*

Maggie laid the ice pack on the table. "You're probably right, Officer Yazzie. I'm just really worried about Terri. There was a lot of blood on the floor beside her."

The screen door squeaked open, and Officer Yoyetewa stepped into the kitchen, followed by a paramedic, who knelt in front of Maggie and did a quick exam of her jaw. "You should have that ex-rayed, ma'am. You could have a fracture."

"Thank you. I might do that if it gets any worse."

"Your choice. We're taking Miss Mitchell into the ER right now."

"Yes, I'll follow behind in my car to be there with her." She stood up, pulled Nathan's jacket from her shoulders and handed it to him.

"You'd better keep that on for now. Your clothes are still wet, and you don't want to catch a chill."

"Thank you, Officer." Maggie grabbed her purse and rummaged through it, searching for her car keys. She shoved her hands into her jeans pockets. "Oh, no. I can't find my keys. Can this day get any worse?" She plopped down in the chair and held her head in her hands.

"Don't worry, Miss Beaumont. I can transport you to the hospital to be with Miss Mitchell."

The wind rattled the trailer's thin walls. Something told Nathan the storm raging outside was nothing compared to the one brewing around Maggie Beaumont.

Chapter Two

Maggie slid into the front seat of Officer Yazzie's car, her wet shoes squeaking on the rubber floor mat. Her face warmed, embarrassed to need a lift back to camp from the hospital. She'd already taken up hours of his time. Doctors had admitted Terri for observation with a mild concussion, and it was determined Maggie had no fracture to her jaw.

Nathan started the cruiser, wrapped a strong, bronzed hand around the gearshift, and turned his intense gaze on Maggie. Something that might have been a smile lifted one side of his full mouth. "Okay, Miss Beaumont, are we taking you back to your campsite at Canyon de Chelly?"

"Yes. And again, Officer, I'm so sorry. I must have lost the keys to the Jeep when I was on the floor next to Terri." Her eyes misted over, and then she turned to face the window. "I am so grateful she'll be okay. What happened to her was scary. She could have died. Or, for that matter, I could have."

His voice softened. "Yeah, I'm glad you're both okay. And it's not a problem. Just let me update dispatch, and we'll be on our way." After a quick exchange with Officer Nez as to his location and plans to take Maggie home, he put the car into drive, turned out onto Route 7, and headed west.

Maggie relaxed against the seat. The car had a pleasant smell of coffee, some kind of musky aftershave, and what was probably leftover French fries.

"We'll have you back at your camp soon." He shot her a glance. "Hey, would you mind very much if we stopped off at my mother's place? It isn't really out of the way. I promised her I'd drop off her mail. It won't take long."

"No, not at all. I'm in no hurry." She grinned. "My only concern is that my poor director, Bruce, won't get the Dr. Pepper I promised to pick up for him."

Nathan's friendly laugh filled the car. "Well, we can probably take care of that, too."

Maggie breathed a sigh of relief. "That'll definitely help. I was not looking forward to the conversation I'll have to have with him. 'Hey Bruce—I have to tell you Terri was hospitalized with a concussion, and, by the way, I lost the keys to one of the university's Jeeps.' I was hoping to grease the skids with a little gift."

They drove a few miles west and Nathan made a left across another cattle-guard onto his mother's land. Maggie turned to him. "Oh, this is really close to my father's place."

He nodded. "Yeah, your dad and my mom were neighbors."

"Really? That's a coincidence." She gazed out the window again. "I've noticed that every driveway has a cattle guard near the road. I'd never thought about it before, but I guess they are indispensable out here, aren't they?"

"Sure. Sheep will wander anywhere. And you might have noticed the reservation has wild horses running free—even on residential streets sometimes."

"Yes, I noticed that. I had to stop my car and let horses pass in front of me the first time I drove through town." She chuckled. "And there are horse droppings everywhere."

He shook his head. "Yeah, it's a problem here on the Navajo Nation. Since the cost of feed has risen so much, a lot of ranchers have simply let their horses roam free."

"Incredible."

They drove on in companionable silence, broken only by the occasional squawk of the police radio and the windshield wipers, now on intermittent speed.

Off to her right, Maggie spotted a woman on horseback moving toward them.

"Oh, look! Someone's herding their sheep."

Nathan gave a light laugh. "Yes, that looks like Aunt Shirley. She's bringing the Churros in for the evening." He slowed the car to a stop and reached an arm across her, pointing out the window. "Look. That's Nizhoni Girl, our sheepdog, running alongside. She thinks she's a Churro, too, and stays with the flock all the time. She's not a pet."

"Where are they coming in from?"

"I think Aunt Shirley probably had them out in the west pasture. There's a lot of sage growing out there right now." He lifted an eyebrow. "You know that old saying is true—you are what you eat. When we feed them sage, it gives the meat a better flavor."

Maggie felt a rush of excitement. The fresh air? The sheep? Or was it the man?

Nathan continued down the hard-packed road, the car splashing through rain puddles. As they drew near a small white house, chickens squawked and scattered in every direction. Behind the house loomed the ever-present view of the Lukachukai range with its gentle rust and yellow ridges. As he braked and parked the car, she spotted a weaving loom under a brush arbor, and farther off to the rear, a domed, earthen structure.

Nathan pointed to the hogan. "My brothers and I built it ourselves when we were teenagers. It's a female hogan—it was our home for years."

"Female?"

"Yes, there are two kinds of hogans. Male hogans are for ceremonial purposes. The Navajo believe many things come in twos—the male and the female. This soft rain is a female rain, gentle and nurturing. The thunderstorm was male. It's all about harmony."

Maggie's heart thumped. "Seriously? You helped build that? This is all so beautiful." She craned her neck and took it all in. *This is my father's culture. A culture so very different from the one I grew up in.*

"Come on. Meet my mother. After all, you're neighbors now."

Maggie stepped out of the car, a sudden shyness overtaking her as she strode toward the house. She brushed her hands down her wrinkled, still slightly damp shirt. *I must look like a complete wreck with my bruised face and messy hair. What in the world will she think of me looking like this?*

A petite, dark haired woman came through the door smoothing out a long skirt and a dark blue velvety shirt, cinched at the waist with a silver concho belt. At her neck was a silver and turquoise necklace. She wore her white-streaked black hair pulled back into a bun and fastened with a yarn hair tie.

Nathan bent close to Maggie's ear. "She dressed up for company. I told her we might stop by. By the way, she speaks very little English."

Maggie swallowed hard.

Nathan gestured from Maggie to his mother. "This is my mother, Wanda Yazzie. She is from the Red Running into the Water People Clan, born for the Coyote Pass People Clan."

Wanda nodded. "*Ya'at'eeh*."

Nathan spoke to his mother and nodded to Maggie, introducing her.

Maggie felt her forehead wrinkle in confusion.

Nathan turned to her. "Navajo people always explain their *k'e*, or clans, when they meet others. It indicates the kinship between us. When you meet someone you share a clan with, you are family."

"Oh, that's beautiful."

Nathan addressed his mother, and upon hearing him mention John Adakai, Wanda's face lit up with surprise and delight.

He translated back to Maggie. "My mother says she's happy she'll be neighbors with the daughter of her friend, John Adakai. She says you have the same eyes."

Maggie's heart swelled with pride, and she felt a smile spread across her face.

"My mother would like you to come in for a glass of tea."

"Alright, I'd love one."

She followed Wanda and Nathan into the little house. Christian images covered the walls. A tapestry depicting the Last Supper hung over the sofa. She shot a glance at Nathan.

He shrugged. "Consequences of the Bureau of Indian Affairs boarding schools."

Wanda stole a look at the tapestry, turned back to Maggie, and said something. Nathan translated.

"She said her friend John walked the Jesus Road and so does she."

~

Maggie unbuckled her seatbelt as Nathan pulled up in front of the trading post.

"Here's your chance to pick up your director's soda."

She tilted her head. "Aren't you coming in, too?"

"Sure, I'll come in with you." He stepped out of the car and led the way up the stairs of the old stone and adobe building. A bell jingled as the door opened. The smell of herbs, woolen blankets, and leather goods teased her nostrils.

A young Navajo man strode out of the back room and came around the counter. "Ya'at'eeh, Officer Yazzie."

"Ya'at'eeh, Dan Hoskie." Nathan nodded at Maggie. "This is Maggie Beaumont. She's part of the archeological dig going on at Canyon de Chelly. She's also the daughter of John Adakai from out on Highway 7."

Dan's eyebrows shot up at this piece of information. "You don't say? Now that's quite a coincidence."

Maggie stepped closer to the counter. "Yes, John Adakai was my father. He left his mobile home to me, and I'm trying to decide if I want to keep it or maybe sell." She smiled. "I'm kind of leaning toward keeping it. I like it out there."

Dan dropped the cartons of cigarettes he'd brought in from the storeroom and fumbled to pick them up. "You like it out at that old place?"

"Yes. It's so beautiful out there."

Dan chuckled. "Nothing out there but rattlers and scorpions. Why would a nice young lady like you want to live there?"

Maggie felt the smile slip from her face. "You know, I haven't really made up my mind."

Dan cleared his throat, then turned to Nathan. "So, Officer Yazzie. I heard you all arrested a couple of bikers the other day."

Nathan nodded. "Yes, two of them."

Dan leaned over the counter. "Seems that's been happening a lot lately."

"Yeah, they usually stir things up here in Chinle on their way to the biker rally in Sturgis, but that's not until August." Nathan shrugged.

"They sure cause a lot of trouble."

Maggie felt a chill run the length of her spine. *Could it have been one of these bikers who attacked Terri and me?* She shook her head and grabbed a six-pack of Doctor Pepper. *I can't let this get the better of me.* She sat it on the counter, and Dan rang it up.

He shot a stiff smile down at her. "Thanks for coming in today. Glad to meet you, Maggie."

~

Weariness hit Maggie hard as Nathan pulled the NNPD cruiser into the campsite at Canyon de Chelly. The sun's last rays beamed over the small group of trailers she and the rest of the team would call home for the next few weeks.

"Thank you so much for everything you did today. I loved meeting your mother." She shook her head. "This day has been an incredible mix of good and bad experiences. I think later this evening, I'll need to call the nurses' station and check on Terri."

Nathan leveled his warm, dark gaze at her. "I'm glad you enjoyed stopping by my mother's place. She likes you. She said she sees your father in you and you have the same spirit."

A sensation of pride and affection for a man she'd never met welled up in her chest. "Thank you, Officer Yazzie. That means more to me than you know."

He perked up. "Oh, and while we were in the trading post, I got a call from my recruit. He found your car keys in the shed where you were kneeling by Miss Mitchell."

"Thank goodness! I thought Bruce would have my hide for losing those."

Nathan laughed. "Well, maybe you should butter him up first with the Dr. Pepper."

"That's the plan." She stepped out of the car and opened the rear door to retrieve her grocery bag. A small gasp escaped her, and she slapped a hand to her forehead.

"What's wrong?"

"I can't believe it. I forgot to bring the box of my father's belongings. I wanted to go through them more carefully tonight."

Nathan's eyes went wide. "Get in the car. I'll run you back out to get it."

"Oh, no. That would be way too much trouble, but thank you for offering." She lifted the grocery bag into her arms.

"Well, I have a couple of meetings tomorrow, then I can be here to pick you up at about ten o'clock. We'll go out to your place and get your vehicle." He paused. "I mean, if that's okay with you." He looked almost boyish with his black hair windswept across his dark skin.

Maggie looked at the ground. Bruce could have easily taken her to do that, but the idea of going with Officer Yazzie was much more appealing. "Alright, thank you. Ten o'clock it is. See you then."

"Goodnight, Miss Beaumont."

~

The next morning, Nathan pulled open the door of the Chinle police station, nodded to Officer Leslie Tsosie, and strode into conference room C.

Mervin Yoyetewa sat waiting for him, his ankle crossed over his other knee, nervously shaking his foot. He jumped to his feet when Nathan entered the room.

"Have a seat, Yoyetewa." Nathan tossed a pad of paper onto the conference table and sat down.

"You passed the academy, you know the basics, and I won't waste time with it. You know what to expect from the job. Let's cut to the chase and talk about yesterday."

Yoyetewa picked up a pen and worried it between his fingers. "Yes, sir. Well, after you left, Detective Deschene's unit arrived, and we did a general search of the area. The primary item of interest was a broken chair leg found outside of the shed. It had traces of blood on it." He gave a small smile. "I'd mark it for the weapon used against Terri Mitchell."

Nathan nodded and kept his gaze level.

Yoyetewa cleared his throat. "After Detective Deschene and I secured the scene, I noticed that, out of the dozens of crates in the shed, one of them right next to where Ms. Mitchell had been laying was open. I glanced inside. It looked like archeological artifacts—I guess old Mr. Adakai was a collector or something—but Ms. Beaumont's keys had fallen inside." He reached into his pocket and produced the keys. "I grabbed them for her."

Nathan reached out and took them from his hand. The dark-eyed beauty flashed through his mind. "I'll take these to her myself. Go on."

"Detective Deschene photographed the inside of the shed, but when I was fishing out Ms. Beaumont's keys, I noticed the crate was full of a lot of pottery pieces—potsherds, I guess they call them. Also, a couple of cool old stone fetishes and what not. I only glimpsed them, but it looked like one was an alabaster wolf. They looked ancient. I can't believe Mr. Adakai just left them out in that shed."

Nathan's brows furrowed. "And, of course, Detective Deschene got pictures of the contents of this box?"

"Yeah. He didn't take things out of the crate, but he took a couple of photos looking straight down into it."

Nathan pushed away from the table and stood. "Good. I need to follow up with Deschene, but we'll talk tomorrow. You stay on this."

Nathan strode out of the conference room and into the common office space lined with desks. He approached Joe Deschene, who looked up at him over the rim of his paper cup of coffee.

Nathan stood over Deschene's desk, folded his arms and frowned down at him. "Detective, we have coffee makers all over this precinct with pots of great coffee. Why in the world do you drink that nasty vending machine stuff?"

Deschene scowled. "What do you mean, nasty? I love this coffee. I've always drunk it. I just drop my quarter into the machine and get a cup of hot, fresh brew."

Nathan shook his head. "Whatever you say."

Without another word, Deschene pushed a manilla file folder at him. The veteran cop ran a hand through his gray-streaked hair and took a sip of his coffee. "I made a copy for you. Figured with your rookie there and you being first on the scene, you'd want to stay in the loop. Look it over and we'll talk later."

Nathan gave a nod. "Appreciate it." He picked up the file and turned to see Lieutenant Benally in front of his office door across the room.

Deschene muttered under his breath. "Looks like the lieutenant wants to talk with you."

Nathan swallowed a sigh and kept eye contact. "It appears so."

Squeezing between desks and file cabinets, Nathan reached his uncle's side. "Ya'at'eeh, Uncle Ben." He pasted on a weak smile.

The lieutenant's eyes softened around the edges, but his voice remained stern. "We've got a situation with looting of artifacts at the Adakai property near Canyon de Chelly. Your rookie, Yoyetewa, made an interesting find yesterday. Follow up on that and see where it leads."

Nathan fought to keep his face unreadable. *Possible stolen artifacts at a dead man's house.* "Right, Uncle Ben."

He strode toward the double front doors. "I already hate this case."

~

Nathan swapped his gear from the Crown Victoria cruiser he'd been driving to a NNPD Tahoe SUV. The back roads had already taken a toll on the car he'd driven yesterday.

Canyon de Chelly stretched out in pale layers as he pulled into the dig site. He rolled up in front of the cluster of trailers, unsure of which door to knock on first. Maggie saved him from having to make that choice as she exited the nearest one and walked towards him, her long, dark ponytail swaying in perfect rhythm with her stride. She walked toward him with purpose, but something about her pace was off—too quick, maybe, or too measured.

Nathan stepped out and swung her door open before she reached it.

"Good morning, Officer Yazzie." She looked the SUV over and nodded with approval, settling into her seat. "Decided on something with a little more oomph, I see."

He climbed in and closed his door with a thud. "Yeah, with that access road of yours, I didn't want to have to call a tow truck to haul us back to the station."

They pulled out onto the highway and headed toward Indian Route 7. The sky was a radiant blue after yesterday's rain, the sun already heating the windshield.

Nathan shot her a sidelong glance. "You want to stop for water? Trading post's our last shot."

"No, thanks. I've got some." She patted the tote bag at her feet.

Nathan lowered the volume on the crackling radio.

Maggie resettled herself in her seat and ran her palms up and down her jeans. She twirled the chain of her necklace in her fingers, twisting and untwisting it.

Nathan lifted the rim of his sunglasses. "Are you okay this morning, Miss Beaumont? You seem a little unsettled."

She inhaled deeply and blew out a long sigh. "Yes, I'm okay. Just thinking about Terri and…thinking about the person who attacked us. Why was he out in the shed? There were more valuables in the home. My dad's three-hundred-dollar western boots, the TV, jewelry. I'm sorry, but he didn't seem like a petty thief."

"Well, the investigation is just getting started. I guess we'll see what turns up." Nathan blew into his hot coffee. "So, have you thought about what you're going to do with your dad's property?"

Maggie gazed out the window. "You know, I'd really like to keep it. The view off the back porch is amazing, and it makes me feel somehow closer to my dad." She smiled faintly, but her eyes stayed guarded.

"But…" She trailed off, fidgeting with the zipper on her tote bag. "At the same time, what happened there makes me… a little leery."

He caught the hesitation in her voice, the way she wouldn't meet his gaze. "You don't have to downplay it. That wasn't just a scare—you were attacked."

She lifted her shoulder in a half-shrug. "I know. I kept hearing Terri's screams in my head all night." She stopped, swallowed hard. "But I want the place to be more than a bad memory, you know? It's what I have left of my dad. I want to be there, to be as close to him as I can be."

"You thinking of staying out there by yourself?"

"I'm used to living alone." She smiled weakly. "Maybe I'll get a guard dog."

Nathan didn't return the smile. "A dog won't stop a man with a knife."

She didn't answer.

She reached in her bag for a bottle of water. "So, Officer Yazzie, I'm curious about your new trainee. I heard you say he is Hopi. I always assumed they only allowed Navajos on the Navajo Nation Police."

"Oh, no. We have a fair number of Hopi officers. The Hopi reservation sits square in the middle of the

Navajo Nation. They're good people." He shrugged. "Anyone that's qualified can join the police force."

"Wow, I had no idea."

They came into the outskirts of town and passed a chain-link fence surrounding the local church. Maggie craned her neck, watching it vanish behind them.

"Why's the gate locked like that?"

"Churches are always targets for vandalism and thievery on the rez—copper wiring, sound systems. The fence helps."

"That's sad." When he didn't respond, she turned to him. "Your mother mentioned both she and my father walked the Jesus Road. I assume she meant they were both Christians. You said that was a consequence of the BIA boarding schools."

Nathan hesitated. "Do you know anything about the history of those places?"

"I've heard a few things. I know they took the children and made them live at the schools."

"Right. And there was a lot of abuse." His hands gripped the steering wheel. "They didn't even allow them to speak their own languages. My uncles can tell stories that would make your hair stand on end." His shoulders tensed. "But it wasn't as bad an experience for everyone. My aunt did fine at the school in Phoenix." He sat silent for a moment. "They just took so much from us."

He felt Maggie's eyes on him. "I don't know what to say."

"There's really nothing to say." He turned his face to her. "How about you? Do you walk the Jesus Road, too?"

She watched the passing scenery, then answered slowly. "I'm a believer. Yes. I guess I've never really committed myself to it, but I *do* believe." She folded her arms. "I wish I could communicate with your mother. I have so many things I'd like to ask her."

"Like I said, she likes you. I'm sure she wishes she could have a conversation with you, too."

The SUV bounced over the cattle guard, and they started up the bumpy road to Maggie's mobile home.

But, after we found those artifacts on your property, you're not the only one with questions about your dad.

~

Nathan followed Maggie up to the door of the mobile home, his boots crunching on the gravel. She moved ahead of him, her posture tight, shoulders pulled in, like she was bracing against something invisible. He walked inside and surveyed the dim interior. The air was stale, heavy with the scent of dust. The walls with their dark paneling swallowed the light, broken only by a few splashes of faded color.

"Let me look around to be sure nobody's been in here."

Maggie nodded stiffly, chafing her hands up and down her arms, fighting off a sudden chill. "I hadn't thought of that." Her voice cracked on the last word. "Yes, please."

He started toward the kitchen and bedroom to check things out. He moved slowly, feeling the weight of her anxiety.

When he returned to her, Maggie stood by the open back door, staring outside with unfocused eyes.

"Miss Beaumont, everything is fine." He looked out at the distant Lukachukai mountains, their jagged peaks catching the early morning sun. The fresh scent of sagebrush reached his nose. "I never get tired of that scent." He kept his tone light, aiming for normalcy.

Maggie nodded. "I can see why. There's nothing else like it."

She headed to the kitchen table, stopped beside the box of keepsakes, and snatched it up. "I'm going to put these in the Jeep before I forget them again."

Nathan took her car keys from his pocket and tossed them to her. "I'll go take another look in the shed."

The outbuilding crouched in the distance, just as he remembered it, still and watchful. He eased the door open, hinges groaning like a warning. A wave of stale air hit him. The interior looked just like Deschene's photos—but colder somehow. Emptier.

Concrete floor. Metal shelving. Crates sagging under the weight of artifacts. Everything sat where it had been, and yet something felt…off.

He swept the shadowy interior with his flashlight before looking at the relics.

"I don't need training to know these are old," he murmured, crouching down. The shards were bone-dry, their painted lines ghosted by time.

Nathan turned with a scowl. Something about this place made his skin itch.

The flashlight flared against something beneath the far worktable. He crouched, breath catching in the stale air. *Still, something—any clue—would be nice.*

He pulled a bag from his belt and scooped the object in carefully, instinctively avoiding contact. Under the flashlight's beam, a small alabaster wolf stared back at him—its eyes hollow, mouth frozen mid-snarl.

"That's amazing."

Nathan jolted upright, barely clearing the underside of the table.

Maggie stood in the doorway, a small frown tugging at her lips.

He stood up straight. "Yeah. Can't imagine how old all of this is."

She approached him and took the wolf fetish so she could examine it. "This is ancient. Possibly Anasazi." Her gaze flicked down to the rest of the crates, then back to him. "This should be in a museum, or a tribal archive—not here."

Nathan hung his head. "Yeah. Looting's a felony. And this stuff... it's not just illegal. It's sacred."

Maggie's eyes went wide. "No. Surely not. My father wouldn't be a looter. I won't believe that."

"And yet, Miss Beaumont." He gestured to a crate on the worktable. "My rookie, Yoyetewa, found this yesterday." He put the wolf fetish in his belt, then covered one of her hands with his. "I get it—you want to believe he wouldn't do this. But we have to follow the leads. I mean, you've never met John—"

Maggie jerked her hand away and backed toward the door. "Oh, I know where you're going with this. You're already trying to pin something on my father."

Nathan put his hands up in a defensive posture. "Don't jump to conclusions. But I have to take this in for evidence."

She stormed to the door, then froze in her tracks and looked over her shoulder at Nathan. "Actually, there's more." She let out a resigned laugh. "I found something out back of the mobile home."

His pulse quickened. *More?* "What did you find?"

Maggie threw a wave over her shoulder and trudged across the property, Nathan at her heels.

The well-worn path led beyond the shed and down a slight incline where a dry creek bed striped the land. What appeared to be her father's attempt at growing vegetables lay near the creek. There was the remnant of a tilled garden bed where he'd grown something— probably corn and beans.

Further back, near the base of a secluded outcropping of rocks, Maggie pointed to freshly turned soil. She knelt by a distinct rectangular area. The soil had been marked and gridded with methodical care. A string line sagged between two stakes. Someone had been working here. Not a hobbyist. Someone who knew what they were doing had been excavating in this spot.

Over near a scrubby pinyon tree, Nathan spotted a small sifter.

His stomach tightened. He crouched beside her. "Is this…?"

Maggie ran her hand through the loose dirt. She lifted it to show Nathan a shard of broken pottery.

"Yes, someone's started their own dig site here. Someone's looting artifacts."

Chapter Three

Maggie brewed a cup of tea and settled into bed with the box of treasures from her father's mobile home. After the hot day, the desert temperature had dropped and left her room chilly. She took a sip, enjoying how the aromatic steam washed over her face.

She shuffled through the contents of the box, finding more pictures, some cassette tapes, a VHS, and a rubber-banded stack of unopened letters. All addressed to her mother's maiden name, Jaqueline Anderson, and all marked return to sender. Maggie felt the air go out of her.

This was amazing. Beyond anything she'd ever expected to find.

Digging a little deeper in the box, her hand found more treasure—a pouch containing two necklaces. One, a silver cross inlaid with mother-of-pearl, and a hand-crafted silver and turquoise squash blossom necklace. The back of both necklaces bore the etched name of the artisan. John Adakai.

As she held the packet of letters marked *return to sender*, she carefully selected the one with the oldest postmark, curious about its contents. Still, she couldn't shake the feeling that she was intruding in her father's personal space.

Once again, she retrieved the picture of her parents and studied his image. He was handsome—tall and slender, with black hair flowing past his shoulders. *Easy to see why Mom had been drawn to him.* He had an arm wrapped around her shoulders and held her close to his side. They looked to be very much in love.

Maggie drew a breath and carefully slit the envelope open.

February 10, 1999

Dear Jackie,

Hi Babe. I've tried calling you every day. We need to talk out our problem and find a solution. It hurts to think of you so far away with our little one on the way. Let's get things settled between us.

I know you didn't enjoy life on the reservation. It's a much slower pace than what you're used to. I know you had career ambitions. We both did. But I've chosen the Jesus Road. I know it to be the correct way. I must stay here as a witness to my people. They need me.

Jackie, I haven't had a drink for two weeks, and I'm done with that lifestyle. I'm on a fresh path now. I want you and our child here with me. I want you to walk this road with me.

All my love,

John

Maggie looked at the picture of her parents again, and a tear slid down her face. It hurt to think her mother hadn't bothered to read these words. Fresh anger welled up in her heart. If her mother had made a different choice in 1999, a loving father could have raised her. A father who could have taught her to craft traditional

Navajo jewelry, to speak the Dine' language. She might have watched her grandmother weave rugs in the ancient way. She might have had the chance to learn about the Jesus Road her father and Mrs. Yazzie spoke of so fervently. So much loss. So many missed opportunities.

She took a sip of her tea and opened the next letter.

Jackie, please answer my phone calls. I love you and want you here with me. We need to raise our child together...

Maggie read through three of the letters, all saying much the same things. Her father, John Adakai, loved her mother and wanted to be with her, but he'd found a new mission in life. He no longer wanted the corporate position in Albuquerque. He'd found a higher calling among his people on the Navajo Nation.

The fourth letter blurred before her eyes as sleep overtook her.

~

Maggie woke up the next day with the sun beaming on her face, her father's letters still on the bed beside her. She glanced at the clock. Seven-thirty. Now she was in a foul mood. Running late for work at the dig site, she jumped into the shower, but her mind still fixated on the letters she'd read the night before.

With warm water beating down on her shoulders, her thoughts raced through all the events of the last couple of days. It was clear Officer Yazzie suspected her father of criminal activity because of the crate he'd found in the shed. Maggie couldn't deny it was suspicious, but she knew enough about her father now that she doubted he was a looter of Anasazi artifacts.

But how do I prove that?

As she toweled off and threw on fresh clothes, she came to a decision. After work, she'd head out to Mrs. Yazzie's place. Her son, Nathan, had said his aunt went to school in Phoenix. Maybe she could speak English and interpret for them. Maggie was going to try. She needed to learn more about her father, John Adakai. Officer Nathan Yazzie might be tall, dark, and handsome, with a laugh that made her smile just thinking about him, but he would not railroad a dead man into the role of a looter of ancient artifacts. Not if she could do anything about it.

Maggie flew out the door of her trailer and jogged to the dig site. She was relieved to see Bruce and Terri exiting a vehicle. Maggie stared in horror at the bandage wrapped around her friend's head. They paused their conversation and smiled as Maggie approached.

"Maggie! We were just speaking about you." Bruce put a hand on her shoulder and pulled her into the huddle.

Maggie turned to her friend. "Terri. Can you ever forgive me for what happened to you at my place? You could have died."

Terri grabbed Maggie's hand. "No, I won't listen to you talk this way. What happened at your property is not your fault. The intruder knocked you unconscious, too."

Bruce nodded. "Exactly. Maggie, promise me you won't go back out there. You need to stay far away from that old mobile home. It's no place for a woman to be hanging around. It isn't safe." Intense concern darkened his gray eyes. "Promise me."

Maggie gazed from Terri to Bruce and slowly nodded. Of course, she wouldn't tell him she was considering keeping the old ramshackle mobile home. Or that she had every intention of going to visit Officer Yazzie's mother and aunt as soon as she finished her day's work here at the dig site. Safe was a relative term.

~

Maggie flipped on the blinker and slowed for a left turn as she approached the long dirt drive leading to Wanda Yazzie's little white house. The last time she'd made this drive, Nathan had been behind the wheel beside her, pointing out the beautiful landscape and features of his family's home. *Amazing how quickly I became comfortable with him.*

Now, butterflies fluttered in her stomach the closer she got. What would Mrs. Yazzie think of her showing up uninvited? Maggie clutched the box of fancy herbal tea she brought as a gift—just in case Officer Yazzie's aunt Shirley wasn't around.

When she reached the house, she spotted Mrs. Yazzie at work weaving under the brush arbor. She'd seen the beautiful, intricate Navajo rugs hanging in the trading post, many selling for thousands of dollars. It was an ancient art that was nearly lost, just like the crafting of Navajo jewelry. Most so-called Native crafts were now manufactured in other countries.

Mrs. Yazzie stood up from her position in front of the loom and came to the edge of the arbor, a smile on her face. "Ya'at'eeh, Maggie Adakai."

Maggie's heart skipped a beat. She'd called her by her father's last name. Maggie Adakai. She loved it.

"Ya'at'eeh, Mrs. Yazzie." Maggie returned her greeting and the warm smile. She glanced under the arbor and gestured to the rug on the loom. "This is so beautiful. I'd love to know how to weave."

From the door of the house, a rich female voice rang out. "It's a Chinle rug. Our traditional colors are gold, yellow, tan, and terra cotta. You have to start learning to weave pretty young to know how to weave a rug like this."

Maggie turned to the woman speaking and recognized Officer Yazzie's Aunt Shirley. She heaved a sigh of relief. *Thank goodness! This couldn't have gone any better.*

Shirley stepped out into the yard and came under the arbor, waving Maggie over. "A really good weaver can make a rug so tight it will hold water."

"That's so amazing." Maggie shook her head in wonder. Once again, a feeling of loss and deep resentment filled her.

She held out her gift of tea. "I brought this for you both. I hope you like it."

Wanda spoke to Shirley, who translated. "Let's go inside and brew the tea. We can talk for a while."

Maggie followed the two women inside to the kitchen with its yellow walls. Wanda moved efficiently through the room, setting water to boil while Shirley seated Maggie at the table.

Maggie twisted her hands together in front of her. "Thank you for inviting me in. To be honest, I was hoping we could talk about my father. Since Mrs. Yazzie and he were friends, and since there's so much I never got to learn, I just hoped..." Maggie's face heated, and she gave a small shrug. "I guess I hoped you could help me get to know him a little better."

Shirley nodded and translated to Wanda.

Mrs. Yazzie came to the table, carrying three cups of tea, then settled into the seat across from Maggie, cradling her cup. With a faint smile, she stared down into her tea, then began speaking. She ended with a sigh and looked up at her sister.

Shirley cleared her throat. "She says, of course, she will tell you about your father. As you know, he and Wanda were neighbors, and they were friends. I got to know him when Ben and I moved onto this property after my sister's husband died. John made very nice jewelry. He met your mother and fell in love. But also... drank more than was good for him in his youth. Then he found the Jesus Road and straightened his path in life." Shirley lowered her eyes. "Still, a man's choices catch up to him. John died far younger than was his time."

Maggie stared into her cup, staggered by the impact of all she'd just learned. She ran her hands over her face, then looked at Shirley. "Did my father have any other relatives? Maybe someone else I could meet and get to know?"

Shirley spoke to Wanda, who shook her head and gave a short reply.

"Wanda says John has a brother somewhere in the area. His name is Thomas, but she hasn't seen him for years and—"

The back door swung open, and Shirley stopped mid-sentence. Maggie looked up to see Officer Yazzie standing in the doorway, his eyes wide.

Nathan glanced around the table from face to face, finally settling on Maggie's. He stepped into the kitchen and closed the door behind himself. "Ya'at'eeh, *Shima'*, Ya'at'eeh, *shima' yazhi*." He nodded at Maggie. "Ya'at'eeh, Maggie Beaumont."

He scraped a chair back and sat down at the table. The space immediately brightened as his energy filled the room. Shirley got up to fix him a cup of tea.

"Nice to see you here visiting with your neighbors. Did Mom and Aunt Shirley get all your questions answered for you?"

Maggie shrugged. "I've only been here for a few minutes. Admittedly, I do have a lot of questions—especially about my father. He's a stranger to me. A man I never knew existed until a little over a week ago." She savored a sip of her fragrant tea. "Your aunt was telling me my father had a brother somewhere in the area."

Shirley glanced at Nathan. "Yes, Thomas Adakai. I believe he lives in Flagstaff, last I heard."

Nathan frowned.

"What is it? Is there something I should know about him? Do you think he wouldn't be happy to hear from me?"

"Oh, it isn't that." Nathan looked up and met her gaze. "I guess you should know the truth. Thomas has always been in trouble with the law. Petty charges, mostly. Spent half his time in lockup in the Chinle jail. I think John was relieved when Thomas decided to move off the reservation."

Shirley sighed. "Yes, Thomas is troubled. Never could just settle down and live a quiet life."

Nizhoni Girl barked in the distance, and Wanda stood and peeked out the nearby window.

Maggie's gaze fell. "And that's all the family my dad had?"

Shirley nodded. "John was divorced. A couple of years after your mother left, he married Anne Begay, and they had a son. Their marriage ended when she left him and moved to Shiprock. I know his son, Luke, sometimes spent summers here with John. That is the only family we know of. Both his parents died, and we don't know of any other kin."

Maggie's hand flew to her face. "A son? So, I have a half-brother? I hadn't even considered that I might have siblings. Wow, I need to digest this information." Her eyes shifted from Shirley to Wanda. "You said he lives in Shiprock, New Mexico?"

Wanda said something to Shirley and she translated. "We're not sure where Thomas and Luke are now."

Maggie smiled, conflicted. "Well, even if I can't track them down, I've met some wonderful new neighbors." *But it would have been great to meet my new family.*

Nathan asked, "So, you're thinking about renewing your father's lease on his land?"

She gazed out the window at the distant mesa. "Oh, I'm definitely thinking about it."

~

Maggie bid Wanda and Shirley goodbye and headed out to the Jeep. Nathan fell into step beside her.

The sun was low on the horizon, and a cool breeze blew a strand of hair across her face.

Nathan opened the door of the vehicle for her as she climbed in, jingling her keys before him. "See? I've still got them."

He closed the door and leaned in the window, his eyes skimming every feature of her face. A slow smile lifted his lips. The scent of his aftershave teased her senses. "I'll be in touch, Miss Beaumont. We'll get the property from your father's shed back to you as soon as possible."

She nodded. "Goodnight, Officer Yazzie."

"You know, since we're neighbors, we should probably be on a first name basis."

"Alright. Goodnight, Nathan." She started the engine.

He slapped the car door, and she started down the long, hard-packed driveway.

As she neared the cattle guard at the end of the drive, Maggie touched her brakes. She felt a certain sponginess as it sank towards the floor. *We need to get these brakes looked at ASAP.*

Maggie made a right-hand turn onto Indian Route 7 and rolled her window down a few inches. The refreshing night air brushed her skin.

Officer Yazzie's face—Nathan's face—still loomed in her mind. She already loved the company of his family. His mother, Wanda, and Aunt Shirley were so warm and friendly, and there was much she wanted to learn from them.

The idea of renewing her father's land lease and staying in his old mobile home still niggled at the back of her brain.

A semi-truck roared up behind her, its headlights glaring in her rearview mirror. She decided to pull over at the next crossroad she came to, so the truck could pass. Seeing a side road ahead, Maggie turned on her blinker and pressed her brakes to slow for the turn.

Her foot went to the floor.

Panic surged through Maggie. Her knuckles turned white as she gripped the steering wheel. The unfamiliar, winding two-lane road stretched before her.

She stomped on the brake, pumping it repeatedly. The vehicle didn't slow down. Her heart thundered, adrenaline rushing through her veins. *I'm going to die.* She fought back tears.

Maggie's mind raced as she searched for a solution. Out of nowhere, she thought of her father, thought of his Jesus Road. *God, please help me! Help me find a way to stop this car.*

The car careened, tires screeching as she took a sharp curve. The speedometer rose — sixty, seventy, eighty miles per hour. She squinted her eyes against the setting sun. The trees flew past, a nauseating blur.

Finally, the road straightened before her, and she spotted a runaway truck ramp. This was her only chance. She yanked on the Jeep's emergency brake with all her might. The car shuddered and tires squealed, fishtailing, as she steered toward the incline.

The vehicle slowed on the sharp uphill grade of the truck ramp. She downshifted to second gear. The Jeep slowed even more. She veered to the left and steered hard to straighten the vehicle.

With every ounce of strength in her body, she pulled the emergency brake again, willing the Jeep to stop. Finally, it skidded to a halt. The smell of burning rubber assaulted her nose.

Maggie dropped her head against the steering wheel, her heart pounding. Her breath came in ragged bursts. Her right arm trembled from the strain of pulling so hard on the emergency brake.

She took a deep shuddering breath, then plopped her head back on the headrest.

With shaky hands, she unfastened the seatbelt, pulled her tote bag from the passenger side floor, and fished around inside for her cell phone.

She dialed 911.

~

Within minutes of receiving the call from the station, Nathan pulled up behind Maggie's Jeep, the lights of his patrol SUV bathing the desert highway in red and blue. He strode to the vehicle and opened her door.

"Maggie, are you okay? Dispatch called me since I was nearby. What in the world happened?"

He reached in, grasped her arm, and helped her exit the Jeep. Her knees buckled, and she fell against him, her legs still unsteady and weak. His arms tightened around her, and she trembled against him.

"I'm sorry. I didn't realize I was so shaky."

He wrapped an arm around her shoulders and led her to the patrol vehicle. "Okay, let's get you inside." He lowered his voice. "Now, start from the beginning. Tell me what happened. This Jeep belongs to the University of New Mexico, doesn't it? I can't believe they'd be so negligent with the maintenance of their vehicles."

Maggie curled up in the passenger seat, her tawny skin pale from the harrowing experience. She wrapped her arms around her knees and a moment later, she answered. "They wouldn't. I've never had trouble with the university's Jeeps. This time, though, the brakes just went. They went straight to the floor. If it hadn't been for that ramp..." She shook her head.

Nathan sighed, leaning one arm against the top of the SUV. His eyes wandered to the Jeep. "I'm going to take a quick look under the hood, okay?"

Maggie gave a quick nod.

Nathan made his way to the vehicle, walking a circle around it. He leaned in the driver's door and popped the hood. Pulling his flashlight from his belt, he clicked it on and held the hood open.

His suspicions confirmed, a coldness built in the pit of his stomach. The brake fluid reservoir was empty.

He let the hood fall closed and tucked away his flashlight. Steeling himself, he walked to his patrol vehicle.

Maggie looked calmer now, her color returned and eyes alert.

"I'm going to call and have someone tow your Jeep into Chinle. I'll drive you back to Canyon de Chelly."

Maggie's mouth quirked. "This is getting to be a pattern."

He allowed himself a small smile. "It is." His mind flashed to Terri lying injured in the shed. *In more ways than one.*

Getting into the car, he called dispatch.

The tired voice of Officer Nez broke through.

Nathan cut her off, speaking quickly in Dine'. *"Can you patch me through to my rookie, Yoyatewa?"*

He pulled onto the highway. His eyes darted to Maggie. He didn't like cutting her out of the conversation, but he didn't want to worry her before he was certain her Jeep hadn't failed on its own.

Brake lines almost never failed on their own.

Less than a minute later, Yoyatewa's voice came over the radio, muffled, clearly talking through a mouthful of dinner.

Nathan cut him off, still speaking Navajo. *"Do you speak Dine'?"*

Yoyatewa hesitated. *"Yes. My mother was Navajo. I can speak some."*

Nathan breathed a sigh of relief. *"Good. Maggie Beaumont's brakes went out on Indian Route 7. I think someone cut them. We need a tow truck. I want you to get on this tonight."*

Yoyatewa's voice brightened. *"Yes, sir. Of course."*

He replaced the radio's mic and forced a smile for Maggie. "I'll call you tomorrow to let you know what happened with the Jeep."

Maggie bit her lip. "Did Officer Yoyatewa suddenly forget how to speak English?" She arched an eyebrow.

Nathan flexed his hands on the wheel and swallowed the guilt rising in his throat. "Why? Because the Navajo Nation Police shouldn't be speaking Navajo on the radio?" He pasted on a smirk. "He'll make sure someone tows your Jeep tonight and checks it out. Gotta keep him on his toes."

~

Nathan paced down the back halls of the Chinle police station, then stopped and leaned against a doorjamb.

He ran one hand through his hair. Two incidents in this case. First with Maggie and her friend Terri, and now a blatant attempt on Maggie's life.

Nathan's heart ached as Maggie's frightened face flashed across his mind. He remembered how she shivered as he helped her to the SUV. She was lucky to be alive after last night.

He made his way to the main workroom. "Yoyetewa," he called. "Get that box of artifacts we collected at the Adakai property and meet me in conference room B."

Minutes later, the rookie came through the door carrying the crate of potsherds and fetishes they'd found in the shed behind John Adakai's mobile home. He set it on the table.

Nathan shoved his hands into his pockets and stared at the box. "We need an actual expert to examine these things. Maybe the manager of that dig going on at Canyon de Chelly. What's his name? Bruce Adams? I think I ought to go have a talk with him. I want him to come in and tell me what he thinks of these relics."

Yoyetewa nodded. "Do you want me to come with you?"

Nathan shook his head. "No, you stay here and keep on this. I'll be back."

After a quick stop at Deschene's desk to get the okay, Nathan was back in the SUV and on the road.

The atmosphere inside the car during the drive back to Chinle PD was thick with Bruce Adams's tension. Nathan walked him into the station, where Detective Deschene waited for them at the front desk.

The detective gave a wan smile. "Sergeant Yazzie, Mr. Adams, follow me."

They headed into a conference room where someone had laid out the recovered artifacts individually across the table. A tape recorder waited in the middle.

"Mr. Adams, we'd like to tape this meeting. Do you give your permission for us to record it?"

Bruce raised his eyebrows. "Sure…I guess so." He signed a consent form and sank into a chair across from them. A *bilagaàna* man in his mid-forties with graying brown hair, he looked every bit the academic.

Deschene hovered over the button on the recorder. "Let's get started."

Adams sat with his hands in his lap, eyes darting between the two lawmen.

"How exactly can I help you, Officer? What do you want my opinion on?"

Deschene leaned against the conference table, arms crossed over the front of his white button-down shirt. The detective's voice was monotone, almost lazy. There was something unshakeable in how he carried himself that Nathan found striking. He knew better than to underestimate the man.

"It's Detective, actually. Joe Deschene. When looking into the assault on your employee, Terri Mitchell, we found these artifacts on the property of the late John Adakai, Maggie Beaumont's father. We have questions about them. We hoped you could examine them and give us your observations." Deschene shrugged. "Anything you notice could be useful."

Bruce Adams widened his eyes and swallowed hard. "Sure. I'll take a look at them."

He put on gloves and began his examination, carefully picking up one piece at a time.

"Looks like the typical artifacts one would expect to find in the Canyon de Chelly area." He held up the alabaster wolf fetish. "This is a beautiful piece. Pueblo. At a glance, about 1200 CE, I'd say."

Nathan and Detective Deschene exchanged glances.

"So, it isn't anything unusual for this region? Not exceptionally old, or from a tribe not usually found in this area?"

Bruce's gaze drifted to the left, avoiding their eyes. "No. Not at all. Just the same as the other artifacts being excavated around the Canyon."

Chapter Four

"Bruce, that Jeep almost got me killed last night." Maggie plopped down at the long picnic table, late again, clutching her coffee mug tight after a night of restless sleep.

Her boss turned to her, a gentle breeze ruffling his hair. "Do you have some sort of jinx where motor vehicles are concerned?" He shot her a wry look.

Maggie fought down a blush. She refused to feel sheepish about the Jeep. This time, it wasn't her fault. "I think you are missing the important part, the part where I said I almost died."

Bruce's smile crumbled. "You're serious." He flattened his hands on the table. "I was just at the police station. Why didn't they tell me? First Terri and now you? Why?"

Terri looked up from her plate of scrambled eggs. "What is it?"

There was a strain in Bruce's voice. "Maggie almost died last night."

Terri scooted over to sit across from her. "What?"

To hide the shaking of her hands, Maggie cupped them around her hot coffee, then blew into it. "The brakes on the Jeep gave out last night. It's a wonder I got the thing stopped." Her voice shook. She gave a weak smile to Bruce. "So, I'll be getting a big raise for this, right?"

Terri snatched Maggie's trembling hand in her own. "Don't you dare joke about this. That sounds awful!"

"Yeah. In fact, I'm waiting to hear back from the tribal police about the Jeep. They towed it into Chinle last night. Officer Yazzie thinks it… might not have been an accident."

Bruce's gaze fell to the table. "Are you sure you're okay?" he whispered.

Maggie lifted one shoulder. "Other than jangled nerves and a sore arm. I'll be fine." She forced a laugh. "I mean, nightmares woke me up about twenty times last night—someone in a dark hoodie climbing in my window, that kind of thing. I finally realized it was just a branch scraping against the glass. In that moment, I felt like running back to Albuquerque. With the morning light, though, I'm more determined than ever to stay."

Her phone buzzed in her pocket, and she answered it.

Nathan's voice filtered from the speaker. "Maggie, how are you after last night?"

She looked from Bruce to Terri and placed a hand over the phone. "Excuse me, I have to take this."

"Good morning, Nathan. What's the news on the Jeep?"

A faint static came through the line as he paused. "Honestly? Not good. It appears someone tampered with your brakes. It doesn't seem to be from normal wear and tear."

Something in the back of Maggie's mind clicked. Somehow, she had expected to hear this. "It was deliberate."

"Yeah, it looks like it."

An icy shiver ran down Maggie's spine. Her voice tightened. "Who is doing this? And why?"

Her eyes misted up, and she blinked to clear them, accidentally meeting the distressed look on Bruce's face across the table. She ducked her head.

Nathan's voice was steady. "I don't know, but you can believe I will find out."

Maggie released a breath. "When will I be able to pick up the Jeep?"

"It's still being processed. I'll let you know."

"Alright. Well, thanks for calling. I'll talk to you soon."

"Bye." Nathan paused again. "And be careful."

The line went dead. Maggie set her phone on the table and turned to Bruce. "I'm sorry, but could I possibly take the morning off?" She rolled her right shoulder. "My arm's aching, and I don't know how much good I'll be, anyway."

Bruce pointed at her. "You should take the whole day."

Terri ran a hand over the bandage on her head. "What a couple of days it's been. Do you want me to take you to get your shoulder looked at?" She raised an eyebrow. "Or run you to the police station?"

Maggie bit her lip. For all that Nathan had said about the Jeep, he'd withheld even more. And after the conversation he'd had with Officer Yoyetewa the day before, she didn't know if he would tell her everything, anyway. "No, I'm good. I'm sure it's just strained. I can borrow another Jeep. And I already got you injured once this week. I don't want you getting more involved."

Maggie stepped away from the table. She didn't want Terri driving her to the station, but she'd made up her mind. Maggie intended to get some answers.

~

Maggie unlocked her inherited mobile home and entered the now familiar living room. As she flipped the lock on the door handle, a thought struck her. *This flimsy thing is the only barrier between me and a would-be attacker. I should get a locksmith out here to add deadbolts to both doors.*

She tossed her tote bag into the brown Naugahyde recliner in the corner and smoothed the quilt that covered the sofa. With a swift motion, she slid back the olive-green drapes behind the chair, causing a flurry of dust to fill the air.

She dropped a grocery bag of bottled water onto the counter, then stowed them neatly in the old fridge.

For the first time, she took stock of what was in the kitchen. A couple of sticks of butter, a big jar of green olives, a few slices of cheese and old deli lunch meat, which she immediately tossed into the trash can. In the refrigerator door was the usual assortment of condiments, all probably years old.

The cabinets held a few canned goods, beef stew, instant coffee, dog food, and a box of macaroni and cheese. She picked up the can of dog food. So, his pet was a dog and not a cat.

She went to the pet food bowls he kept under the built-in desk and picked up a blue metal bowl with the hand-painted name, "Jimmy".

Well, Jimmy, I hope you went to a loving home.

Gravel crunched in the parking area out front. She flinched and dropped the bowl. Her gun was on the other side of the room, in her bag.

Maggie peeked out the window near the door and saw a Navajo Nation Police cruiser pull up. Her heart quickened at the thought Nathan was here and immediately chastised herself for her silliness. The door opened, and Officer Yoyetewa stepped out of the car. Not Nathan, but she smiled as she saw his slender figure.

She opened the door. "Ya'at'eeh, Officer Yoyetewa!"

He made his way up the stairs, a wide grin on his face. "So, I see you're learning the language, Miss Beaumont."

"Well, not exactly." She held the door open and stepped aside so he could enter. "Actually, you just heard the full extent of my knowledge of the Dine' language."

She led the way into the small kitchen. "May I offer you a water? It's all I have here right now, unless you want instant coffee."

"Yes, water sounds great." His eyes landed on the grocery bag by the counter. "Oh, I see you've done a little shopping and whatnot."

"Not really. I brought some bottled water, but I'm kind of wishing I'd done real grocery shopping."

He took the drink she held out and gave her a sharp look. "Why? Why would you want to stock the cabinets? You don't plan on doing any cooking here, do you?"

She pursed her lips. "Oh, I don't know. I'm giving it serious thought." She stepped over to the sink and turned on the faucet. A loud sputtering, hissing, and banging sound filled the room. A stream of rusty liquid poured out, followed by a clear flow. "Well, I'm sure glad I brought water with me."

She turned back to Officer Yoyetewa and rubbed her hands together. "What brings you out today? How did you know I would be here?"

"I tracked you down. I thought you might want to hear the results of the inspection of your Jeep."

Maybe Officer Yoyetewa would be more forthcoming than Nathan had been on the phone. "Of course! What did they find?"

He twisted the top off his water bottle and took a swig. "Your brake lines were definitely cut. It wasn't failure from normal wear and tear."

Maggie leaned against the counter and exhaled a deep breath. "Did they find any fingerprints or anything useful?"

"No, not yet."

Maggie frowned. "But it's confirmed. Somebody really wants to hurt me."

Officer Yoyetewa nodded. "Yes, ma'am. That's why I don't think you should even consider staying here alone."

"So, let whoever it is just drive me out? Why would anyone want to harm me? I only discovered John Adakai was my father a couple of weeks ago. And look around at what he left me. An old mobile home on land owned by the Navajo Nation. I don't get it."

"And don't forget someone's been digging up artifacts right out here in your backyard. We had them examined today by your supervisor, Bruce Adams."

Maggie inhaled deeply. "Okay, Officer Yoyetewa, let's go look around outside. I want to see what's really been happening out there."

He nodded. "Call me Merv, and I was just about to suggest that." He opened the back door and held it for her.

After an hour of scraping and sieving, Maggie had found several more potsherds and a broken piece of turquoise, all of which Merv took into evidence.

Maggie stood up. She swiped dirt from her jeans and pulled a strand of hair behind her ear.

"Okay, Miss Beaumont. I say let's get inside and fire up that window air-conditioner I saw in the living room."

"I'm for that!" When she pivoted to head back to the mobile home, she nearly collided with a young, black-haired man standing behind her.

He stared at her, his eyes unblinking.

Maggie felt a shiver run down her spine. "May I help you?"

Merv moved up to stand beside her.

The stranger spoke. "I saw the police car and stopped to see what was going on. My name is Luke Adakai. John was my father."

Maggie searched the face before her. Dark eyes, straight nose, full mouth. The picture of her father flashed before her inner eye. A lump formed in her throat, and she swallowed hard. "Wow, you look so much like him. So, you're my brother. I always thought of myself as an only child." Hope blossomed in her heart at the prospect of this new relationship.

A wry smile curled the corners of Luke's lips. "Well, half-brother, but yes, I guess so." His eyes shifted to the Jeep and NNPD cruiser parked in front of the mobile home. "I saw the vehicles here while driving by." He waved back to a sedan parked on the private road and Dan Hoskie, the clerk from the trading post, who stood beside it. "My roommate and I stopped to look. I wanted to see who was prowling around my father's property."

Maggie gave a short laugh and crossed her arms. "I was just checking out the mobile home. I still can't believe our father left it to me."

Luke's gaze dropped to the ground, and his lips formed a straight line. "Yes, I heard about that after his death."

She saw the anger on his face. He didn't like the fact that their father had left it to her.

She gestured to Merv. "And Officer Yoyetewa came by to give me some news."

She looked into Luke's eyes, amazed by the resemblance to the photograph of their father. "Sorry, I'm still thrown for a loop. I only found out about you last night and haven't had time to process."

Luke lifted one shoulder. "Dad mentioned you often. The big sister I never got to meet." His eyes scanned the skyline behind Maggie as he spoke, then came to rest on Merv.

"Luke, won't you and your friend come in and visit for a while? I can make some coffee. We can talk and start getting acquainted."

Luke lifted the corner of his mouth again as he met her eyes. "No, thank you. I was on my way to an appointment, and I'm running late."

"Oh, I'm sorry you can't stay." Maggie shifted to give Luke a hug.

He jammed his hands into his pockets and turned back toward his car. "Some other time."

"Sometime soon? I have so many questions. I really want to get to know you."

"Yeah, we'll talk again soon."

He walked over to Dan, then they got into his car and closed the doors.

"Man, what a jerk." Merv locked eyes with Maggie. He watched as the car drove down the gravel road. "Not a very friendly greeting for his newly discovered sister."

She shrugged. "Hopefully, he'll warm up to me." *I'm not gonna let this go. I'll have to think of some way to win him over.*

"Well, I need to return to the station and turn in this new evidence. Do me a favor and go back to Canyon de Chelly." He gave her a pleading look. "Seriously, it isn't safe for you here."

"Thank you for your concern, Merv. I'll think about it. But I have my handgun in my purse, and I know how to use it."

Maggie stared at the distant mesas, remembering her nightmares. "Maybe I'll regret it, but I'm not going back to Canyon de Chelly tonight. Someone is excavating artifacts here, and it's tarnishing my dad's reputation. I have to find out who is behind this."

Merv gave a sigh of resignation. "If you need to, call 911 tonight. If you're able to get a signal when you need it."

~

Nathan stormed out of the police station and slid into his patrol vehicle. *What's wrong with that mule-headed woman? I told her not to stay in that mobile home alone.*

He'd thought his ears were deceiving him when Merv bustled into the precinct and told him what Maggie was up to.

The sun sat low on the horizon when he pulled up in front of her mobile home and pounded on the door.

She pulled it open and greeted him like she'd lived there all her life. "Nathan. Please come in."

He crossed the threshold and planted his hands on his hips. "What are you doing, Maggie? Yoyetewa told me you think you're spending the night here. Haven't you had enough close calls to understand you're in danger?"

She walked into the kitchen. "Yes, Merv already gave me this lecture, but I'm staying. Somebody is digging on this property and trying to kill me. I want to find out who it is."

She pulled a bottle of water from the fridge and poured it into the kettle on the stove. "I have my gun, and I'm a certified marksman."

Nathan rolled his eyes. "There's a lot more to using a gun than just being able to hit a target."

"I plan to be here tonight waiting for someone to show up."

He leaned in toward her and raised his voice. "Oh, no you're not. Let the police handle this. You can't be bait for whatever nut is out there trying to hurt you." He pulled out a chair at the little Formica table and dropped into it. "I'm not leaving you here alone. It's just that simple."

Maggie pushed up the sleeves of her pale blue t-shirt, rummaged through the cabinet, and pulled out a couple of pans. "Okay, Nathan, if you insist. But I want whoever's doing this to think I'm here alone."

She pulled out the box of mac and cheese and opened the can of peas she'd found. "This is dinner. I hope it looks good to you."

"I've had worse, for sure."

He retrieved a couple of mugs from the cupboard and spooned instant coffee into each one.

Maggie nodded to the cabinet. "I saw some canned milk in there. We'll need that."

Soon, they carried their plates and cups of coffee onto the back porch to eat.

She sucked in a deep breath. "I love it here, Nathan. It's so peaceful and there's something almost magical about the Lukachukais." She sipped her coffee and lifted her eyes to the sky. "I've never seen the stars so vivid. There's no light pollution out here." She pointed to the eastern sky. "Look, there's Orion's Belt!"

Nathan crossed an ankle over his other knee and swallowed a mouthful of macaroni. "Yeah, the night sky is magnificent out here. My mother and Aunt Shirley used to tell stories about sitting in their yard and watching UFOs fly over the Pine Nut uranium mine near the Grand Canyon." He watched as Maggie's head jerked around to him, her eyes huge.

"What? UFOs? You're joking, right?"

"No, not at all. It's common here on the reservation to hear stories of UFO sightings." He stared into his plate and scooped up another bite of mac and cheese. "Of course, it's the skinwalkers you really have to watch for when you're sitting outside at night." A slow smile spread across his face. "I wouldn't make a habit of sitting out here alone if you decide to stay."

Maggie stared at him, her face a study in confusion, then fear. She gazed from him to the mesas in the distance. "I've heard of skinwalkers, but I thought they were just mythical creatures." She set her plate on the small table beside her chair.

Nathan shook his head. "Oh, no. If you live here long enough, you'll come to believe in many things you thought were myths." He scooted his chair a few inches closer to hers. "Don't worry. I'm here to protect you tonight." He put a napkin to his mouth to hide his grin.

A whining sounded from near the shed at the back of the yard.

Maggie startled, lurched out of her seat, then ran behind Nathan's chair. "Is it a skinwalker?" she whispered.

Nathan set his food down. "I don't think skinwalkers whine." He stood slowly and touched the service Glock at his side. He walked to the edge of the porch and listened. There it was again. Whimpering. "Didn't you say your father had a dog?"

Maggie hurried to his side. "Yes, there's a bowl under the desk with the name Jimmy on it."

Nathan grabbed his plate and scraped a few bites of food onto the bottom step. "Jimmy. Come and get it! Here you go, boy."

A scraggly brown dog poked its head cautiously from the side of the shed.

"Jimmy, come here."

The skinny dog took a few steps toward them, creeping nearer to the aroma of warm food.

Nathan squatted down. "C'mon, buddy. Come get a bite." He spoke softly and held a hand out to the dog. "Maggie, go get him some more food and water."

She nodded and slipped into the kitchen, mumbling under her breath. "What a day."

Nathan scratched Jimmy behind the ears as Maggie returned with two bowls—one of water and the other the blue "Jimmy" bowl filled with dog food and a dollop of peas on top. She set them down on the porch. Jimmy dug into the food with gusto.

"Poor thing! I guess he's been hanging around here foraging for food ever since my father passed away."

"I'm sure you're right. He's half-starved and really dehydrated."

Maggie squatted down next to Nathan and stroked Jimmy's head.

Nathan looked over at Maggie and pushed back the ever-present strand of hair that hung loose from her ponytail. His fingers accidentally grazed her cheek. "It looks like you've got yourself a dog. Or do you plan to re-home him?"

At that moment, Jimmy ran up to the back door of the mobile home, barked, and scratched on the door.

Maggie laughed. "Clearly, Jimmy believes he's home now. I'd have a hard time sending him away."

She returned to her chair and sat down. "C'mon, Jimmy. I want to finish my coffee before I go in." The dog crept nearer and laid down at her feet, his head on his paws.

"Yep. You've got yourself an old, ugly, brown dog."

"Shhhh! Jimmy heard that. And he's not ugly, he just needs some TLC."

Nathan chuckled. "Yeah, he sure does."

~

Nathan leaned back against the doorframe as Maggie stacked the freshly washed bowls in the cabinet. "Are you sure you wouldn't rather sleep on the sofa?"

"I'm sure. The SUV'll be fine." He eyed the lumps on the ancient couch. "You sleeping in your dad's room?"

She widened her eyes and exhaled slowly. "I guess so, but I don't mind telling you, I have misgivings about it. Heaven only knows when those sheets were last changed." She shivered and rubbed the sides of her arms.

He snapped his fingers. "Hold on. I'm almost sure I saw a couple of sleeping bags in the back of the Tahoe. You could lay it out on the bed and sleep in it."

"Thanks, I like that idea."

Nathan opened the door and made his way to the SUV. He stopped to scan the area and found no signs of anything suspicious, but he felt a tingling sensation on the back of his neck. Sliding into the vehicle, he drove into a thicket of mesquite shrubs near the trailer. After retrieving a sleeping bag, he returned to the mobile home, staying in the deep shadows.

In the living room, Maggie was switching off the table lamps. She looked up as Nathan came in. "Find it?"

He dropped the bedroll into Maggie's arms. "I hope it helps."

"Yes, I think it will." Maggie took the bag and smoothed a hand over it. She glanced up at him. "You know, I was all set to stay here alone, but I was more than a little nervous. To be honest, I feel better having you with me. I'm glad you insisted on staying." She gave a crooked smile. "And Jimmy, too, of course." She glanced over at the brown mutt who'd made himself comfortable in the corner. He looked up at her and wagged his tail when she said his name.

"Yeah, I think it's best I'm here. You shouldn't be alone tonight."

Maggie made her way to the bedroom door and switched off the kitchen light, casting the mobile home into darkness. "Good night."

"Night, Maggie."

Nathan slipped out of the mobile home, locking the door behind him. He stayed in deep shadow and made his way to the SUV by moonlight. He grabbed his jacket and laid it over his chest to stave off the chilliness of the desert night, then reclined his seat a couple of notches and reached for the cup of instant coffee Maggie had made.

"Yuck! How do people drink this stuff?" It didn't matter. He had to stay awake and alert.

Nathan shifted in the seat, his eyes locked on the access road. As the boring hours passed, he muffled his yawns and emptied the bitter coffee.

A glance at the clock on his phone. *One AM. Only four more hours 'til sunrise.*

A strange noise made Nathan jerk his head toward the mobile home.

He heard it again. A sharp bark. Then a slam, snarling, and clawing madly from the front of the mobile home. Jimmy was losing his mind about something.

Nathan unholstered his Glock and sprinted from the SUV toward the trailer. As he dashed for the door, Maggie appeared in the open entrance, gun in hand.

The assailant knelt to one knee and took aim... directly at Maggie.

Adrenaline flooded Nathan's system. He raised his gun to shoulder level and aimed center mass of the would-be shooter.

"Halt! Navajo Nation Police!"

The man turned his face toward Nathan, then jumped to his feet. Instantly, he vanished into the brush beside the drive. Nathan sped after him. Heart pounding, he chased the figure through the dark thicket of brush.

Suddenly, a shot rang out from the darkness at the side of the road, zinging past his shoulder. It thwapped into the paneling of the mobile home, barely missing the door where Maggie had stood.

A short distance down the drive, an engine started, and headlights flashed on, blinding Nathan. A black vehicle roared past him and fishtailed into the darkness.

Chapter Five

Maggie slumped into her dining chair as Detective Deschene finished taking his report. "The team will continue working the scene. Hopefully, after daylight, they'll be able to find any shell casings or other evidence we can't see in the dark."

Nathan stood up. "Thanks, Detective. I'll stay here tonight. I doubt the suspect will be back, but I don't want her to be alone."

Deschene nodded. "I agree. Someone's out to get her, that's for sure."

The detective nodded to Maggie. "You get some rest, ma'am."

"Thank you, I will." Maggie clutched her stomach, her insides quivering like jelly. Outside, a car door slammed. She flinched, the memory of gunshots still ringing in her ears—the awful sound they made as they hit the mobile home right outside her door.

Nathan saw the detective out, locked the door behind him, then whirled on her. Maggie shrank back.

"I told you not to stay here, but I didn't realize I needed to tell you not to stand in the doorway when there's crossfire going on outside. Do you think that if

69

you have a gun in your hand, you're protecting yourself? Do you even know how close you came to being killed?"

"Please stop." She put her hands to her head and rubbed her temples. "You've been telling me off for an hour. I know I made some dumb mistakes, okay?" She folded her arms tightly across her chest. "Can we please drop it now?"

"Yes, we'll drop it, but from now on, we're doing things my way." He softened his voice. "Someone's out to kill you, Maggie." He plopped down on the sofa. "And another thing…I'm gonna teach you to use that gun properly. Right now, I think it's more of a hindrance than a help to you."

Maggie stood and slowly moved towards the bedroom. She stopped at the doorway. "I really am grateful. Thank you."

She looked back at him over her shoulder. "It isn't your job to be my personal bodyguard. I know you're going above and beyond. And I realize I made some foolish mistakes tonight."

Nathan looked down and nodded, some of the tension draining from his face.

She crossed her heart. "I promise, I won't go brandishing my gun again until you give me the okay."

A small smile tugged at his mouth as he walked out the door. "Get some sleep."

~

Bright and early the next morning, Maggie boiled water on the stove, made two cups of strong instant coffee, and put the last of the dog food in Jimmy's bowl.

Nathan stumbled into the kitchen, rubbing his eyes with the heels of his hands. "I could use about three more hours of sleep." He reached for a mug.

"Same here. I feel like I hardly closed my eyes." She sipped her coffee and steeled herself for the reaction she knew she was about to get.

"Nathan, I thought about this all night and I'm going back to Canyon de Chelly to pick up my things. I'm going to stay here until this attacker is found and arrested... I..."

"What? Didn't we just talk about this? You can't stay here."

"Yes, we talked about it, and I meant everything I said. I'll be more careful, and I know I need more training with my gun. But I have to stay here. I've got Jimmy to take care of now, and I need to know who's after me. Surely you must realize there's a deeper reason for what's happening. I think it must be connected to the digging someone's doing here on my dad's property." She looked him in the eye. "You don't still think my father was selling looted artifacts, do you?"

Nathan took a step toward her. "Maggie, please—" He touched her shoulder. "Give up the idea of staying here."

She smiled at him. "Won't you even try to understand? I need to stay here until we find out who is trying to drive me out, and why. It's important to me. If we don't catch this guy, I'll never really be safe here, and I want my father's name completely cleared of any wrongdoing."

Nathan set his coffee down so hard it splashed on the counter. He shook his head. "Why are you so stubborn?"

"I never got to know my father at all, but this feels like something I can do to honor him. I promise I won't get in your way again."

Nathan fixed his eyes on her—angry and exasperated—then determined. "No. Sorry Maggie, but I forbid it. We can probably get an officer in here to impersonate you. We can bait this guy with a trained officer... not an overzealous civilian."

Maggie glared at him.

"How about you come on over to our place this weekend? We're starting sheep shearing. We'll show you how the Navajo really live." He cocked an eyebrow. "Or are you afraid of roughing it for a couple of days?"

She raised her hands in surrender. "Okay, Nathan. I'll come for the weekend. But don't think I'm giving up on trying to prove my father's innocence."

He heaved a sigh of relief. "Okay, we'll talk about that this weekend."

Maggie perked up. "Oh, and I meant to tell you." She took a sip of her coffee. "When Merv was here yesterday, we found more potsherds at the dig site out back. It was odd."

"How so?"

"The piece was very distinct. I'm almost sure it came from a Black-on-White Tularosa pot. I'd guess it came from the twelfth century. We should have Bruce look at it."

"We just had Bruce at the station yesterday, looking at the relics we got from the shed out back. He didn't seem to think there was anything special about them."

Maggie shot an amazed look at him. "Really? That surprises me. He's much more knowledgeable than me, but I'm sure this was a unique piece. And I'm sure it's Anasazi."

~

Maggie jogged behind Nathan as they rushed into the Chinle police station. He led her down hallways and unlocked the door to conference room B, where the artifacts from her father's property still lay on the table.

Maggie put on gloves and picked up a sherd from the collection. She looked up to meet his gaze, her eyes filled with shock and confusion.

Nathan's shoulders tensed. "So, Bruce Adams lied to us?"

"I…" Maggie stopped herself and she schooled her expression. "I would say that these artifacts are consistent with the potsherds Merv and I found yesterday. They're not Pueblo. They're older than what archeologists usually find in the area. I can't even imagine how much they would go for on the black market."

"And the archeologist in charge of your dig just somehow didn't realize this?"

"It seems unlikely, doesn't it?"

The door clicked open behind Nathan.

Officer Yoyatewa edged up to Maggie. "Hey, I was hoping to talk with you today. The garage called. They're done with your Jeep."

Maggie startled at the abrupt change in subject. "Oh. Okay. I have another Jeep right now, but I'm heading back to Canyon de Chelly tonight. I'll ask someone to help me pick it up tomorrow."

A smile spread across Yoyatewa's face. "I could…"

Nathan interrupted. "Well, I need to talk with Detective Deschene about these developments. I'll call you first thing in the morning."

~

An hour later, Maggie pulled up to her trailer at Canyon de Chelly, gravel crunching under her tires, her thoughts still racing from what she'd found out at the station. She opened the back door of the Jeep, allowing Jimmy to hop down and sniff his new surroundings.

"C'mon, boy." Maggie entered her stuffy trailer and turned on the AC, the blue curtains on her window billowing out. She noticed the box of letters she had yet to finish reading sitting on the bedside table. *I'll get back to these tonight.*

She went to the closet, grabbed a quilt, and laid it across the end of her bed. Jimmy immediately hopped up and stretched out on it.

There was a knock at the door. She opened it to find Terri standing there, her blonde hair braided and hanging over one shoulder. "Maggie, did I just see you take a dog into your trailer?"

Maggie invited Terri in and gestured to the scruffy dog, who'd made himself at home.

"Remember the pet dishes at my dad's mobile home? This is the dog that goes with them. Meet Jimmy."

"Is he friendly?"

"Sure, he's been a real sweetheart so far."

Terri sat on the edge of the bed and scratched his neck.

Maggie glanced out the door, then turned to Terri. "Is Bruce in his trailer?"

"Yeah, I saw him go in there a few minutes ago." Terri quirked an eyebrow. "Are you back to stay now?"

Maggie sat down beside her on the bed. "Actually, Officer Yazzie asked me to spend the weekend at his mother's place. They're starting the sheep shearing and he thought I'd be interested."

"Really? That's quite an offer from someone you barely know."

"It turns out Nathan's mother and my dad were good friends." Maggie smiled. "Mrs. Yazzie said they both walked the Jesus Road."

"Wow, that is a coincidence." Terri's face softened. "So, she's just being a kind neighbor?"

Maggie paused and looked down at her hands. "It's a long story. Last night at my dad's mobile home, someone showed up after I went to bed. Nathan was keeping watch in his SUV. He and the prowler exchanged gunfire." She covered her face with her hands. "Like an idiot, I grabbed my gun and stood in the doorway. I thought I'd prepared myself for this, but I wasn't as ready as I thought. The prowler pointed a gun straight at me. If it weren't for Nathan, I might be dead."

Maggie patted Jimmy's back, her hand trembling.

Terri grabbed her wrist to still it. "You're shaking. That must have been terrifying."

"Yeah. I got in a little over my head. Still, I don't want to run from this—I want my dad's name cleared, but Nathan thinks I'm setting myself up as a target. He suggested having an officer pose as me, but I feel the only way we're gonna catch this person is if I'm there, in the mobile home. I'm sure it's the same person who attacked you."

Terri frowned. "You don't mean you're planning to stay there alone?"

Maggie looked down, then nodded. "Yes, I'm thinking about it." She met Terri's gaze. "I'll hold off, though, and go to the Yazzie's for the weekend." She patted Jimmy. "Hey, don't forget…I have a guard dog now."

Terri gave Jimmy a scritch behind his ears. "And speaking of the guard dog, you and me—we're giving him a bath. He seems sweet, but he's dirty. Probably has fleas, too. I think it'll take both of us to get it done."

Maggie sighed. "I guess you're right." She glanced at the box of letters. *Tonight.* She pushed up to her feet. "Alright, Jimmy. Bathtime."

~

Behind the kitchen trailer, Maggie met Terri with Jimmy and a bar of soap. "This was all I could find."

"It'll be fine." Terri struggled to turn the water handle with a pair of pliers. She held the hose in her other hand.

"It'll have to be." Maggie knelt beside the dog, one hand on his collar. She peered into his big brown eyes. "You're going to smell so much better."

As Maggie worked the soap over Jimmy, both women used their free hands to lather his fur.

Bruce's voice carried around the corner of the trailer. "You heard me. I never should have gotten involved in this. It's not worth it."

Terri snapped her head up and caught Maggie's eyes. Maggie gestured for her to stay silent.

Bruce continued, his voice growing louder. "I want out." His tone took on a growl. "I don't care—do what you have to, but I'm getting out of this mess. I'm done."

He went silent and, a few seconds later, a door slammed on the next trailer to her right.

~

Maggie put an enormous green salad in the middle of the long outdoor table, then sat down, with the freshly scrubbed Jimmy on the ground at her feet. Terri followed, balancing a platter of ribeye steaks in one hand, and in the other, a tofu hash. She arranged both on the table for the group's communal meal, then took her seat across from Maggie.

Maggie leaned toward Terri. "How do you keep your health without eating protein?"

Terri set her hands on her hips. "There are plenty of ways to get protein without eating meat—tofu and legumes, greens. And I'm a vegetarian, not a vegan, so eggs, too."

Bruce walked out of the kitchen trailer with a bowl of baked potatoes. The smile slipped from Maggie's face.

Bruce gave her a curt nod, then went to sit at the far end of the picnic table.

Terri locked eyes with her friend and raised her eyebrows. She leaned in toward Maggie, her voice a whisper. "That's not like Bruce."

"I don't know. He's been acting weird lately." She picked up a pitcher of iced tea, filling Terri's glass, then her own.

Maggie turned at the sound of a vehicle rolling down the gravel drive. "Oh. It's Merv with the Jeep. The Chinle police department finished processing it for evidence. Looks like he's bringing it to us."

Merv parked the Jeep and strode up to the table. "Hey, do I have perfect timing or what? Steaks!"

She gestured to the seat by her. "Sit down, Merv. We have plenty of food."

He took a seat, shaking his head. "No thanks, but I will have a glass of iced tea."

"Merv, do you remember Terri?" Maggie gestured to her friend across the table.

"Of course. I hope you're feeling better now, Miss Mitchell."

Terri smiled. "Yes, I feel fine. The headaches aren't bothering me anymore."

Maggie forked a steak onto her plate. Jimmy sniffed the air and whined. "Quiet, boy. If you're good, I'll save the last bite for you." She turned back to Merv. "Are you sure you won't have any dinner?"

Merv took a deep drink. "No thanks. I'm on duty, and I need to get back to the station soon."

Terri's gaze drifted to the Jeep. "Oh? How *are* you getting back?"

Merv's eyes widened, his jaw going slack, the glass halfway to his lips. The three sat in silence for one second, two.

Merv blinked. "Well, uh. That's a good question."

Maggie fought down a laugh. "Should I call Nathan to come pick you up?"

A blush reddened his cheeks. "That, umm, might be for the best. I can't believe I forgot to arrange a ride back to the station."

About the time they finished eating, Nathan pulled up in his Navajo Nation Police Department SUV. He slammed the door shut and shoved his hands into his pockets.

Maggie ran ahead of Merv, hoping to diffuse Nathan's anger. "Hey, you should come sit with us. We have steaks and baked potatoes. They're still warm."

Nathan's gaze remained fixed on Merv, not glancing at her.

Merv slowly approached. He scuffed the toe of his boot in the dirt. "Hey, Sergeant Yazzie. I was going to talk with you about picking me up when that call came over the radio about a domestic disturbance at the Nakai place."

Nathan glared at Merv. "I thought you made it through the police academy. Didn't they teach you any responsibility?"

Maggie gasped. "It was just an accident."

Nathan turned his back to Merv. "Wait for me in the SUV. We'll talk about this when you get back to the station."

His eyes shifted to Maggie. He made his way to the now-empty table and Maggie sat down beside him.

The sun was sinking below the rim of the canyon, sending red tones through Nathan's black hair. He poured himself a glass of tea and twirled it between his hands.

Hard to believe this is the same man. Poor Merv.

"Really, I don't think Merv is irresponsible. He was distracted and trying to help me out."

He looked down into his glass. "Don't defend him, Maggie. Police officers should be held to a higher standard. An officer's every action can make a difference between life and death. It may seem like I'm being hard on him, but if he can't handle this, maybe he's not cut out for the job." He stared at the horizon. "If Uncle Ben were his training officer, he'd be walking back to the station."

Maggie sighed. "Well, I guess you'd know."

Nathan turned to her, inhaled a deep breath and changed topics. "Speaking of my family, I told my mom and Aunt Shirley you're coming this weekend for the sheep shearing. They were both pleased. I think they plan to teach you how to make frybread."

Maggie's face lit up. "I'd love that!"

"You can even bring Jimmy with you." He gave her a sideways glance. "And bring your gun. I'll try to find time to give you a lesson."

She rolled her eyes and looked away. "Oh. That. Yeah, I guess I do need a little practice."

Nathan left the table and strode toward the SUV. "Then I'll pick you up Saturday morning."

~

As Jimmy lay down at Maggie's feet, she settled into bed with a cup of her favorite herbal tea. She pulled the box to herself and took out the next envelope from the stack.

April 2, 1999

Dear Jackie,

While you seem determined to start over in Albuquerque, that doesn't mean we can't keep in touch. I received the divorce papers and saw that our daughter was born—Margaret Ann. It hurts that I wasn't there for her birth. You know I want to be involved with our child, and I still hope we can make things work.

I went to the church on Highway 7 last Sunday. I was hoping Thomas would come with me, but he refused. You never met my brother Thomas, but he considers going to the Christian church abandoning the old ways. For all his flaws, our culture means a lot to him. I still haven't had a drink. You'd be so proud of me.

I've been reading the Bible, especially the red letters, and have been making notes. I wish you were here to go through it with me. It's changed something in me that is hard to explain.

I miss you so much, Jackie. I don't want to give up on a future with you.

Love,

John

A tear streamed down Maggie's face. *John Adakai, I sure wish I could have known you.*

~

Maggie stood waist-deep in a sectioned-off grid, the sun glaring in her eyes as it set in the western sky. A breeze drifted across her face, cooling the sheen of perspiration on her brow. She'd been carefully brushing around the perimeter of an exposed potsherd. As the distinctive design became clearer, she felt the excitement grow in her chest. Anasazi—very similar to the potsherds found on her father's property.

Bruce told law enforcement they weren't excavating anything unusual. Why would he blatantly lie? Anger rose inside her.

Within half an hour, she'd completely uncovered the broken pottery. Maggie carefully extracted it from the earth and held it in her hand. She climbed from the pit, bagged the potsherd, and marched across the compound where she knew Bruce was working with a group of undergrads.

She stood at the rim of the grid, where she found him bent over his work.

"Bruce."

A moment passed as she waited.

"Bruce. I need to talk to you."

He raised up and swiped his forehead with his sleeve. "What is it, Maggie?

"I want to show you something. Could you come up here for a minute?"

He exhaled and climbed out of the pit.

"Sure. What did you find?" He pulled his glasses from his pocket protector and slid them on. "What have you got there?"

"Oh, nothing much. Just what I judge to be a twelfth-century black-on-white Tularosa pot." She paused and stared him down. "Very similar to the sherds we found on my dad's place. You know, the ones you examined at the Chinle police station." She held it out to him. "You lied, Bruce. Care to tell me why?"

Maggie's eyes bored into him, her face burning with anger.

He stared back at her, expression unreadable. "Maggie—"

She shook her head and cut him off. "No excuses."

Bruce's eyes closed for a moment. "No, no excuses." Suddenly, they opened, and he looked around. "But this isn't the place for our conversation." He grasped her elbow and steered Maggie away from the dig site. "Really, we need privacy to talk this out."

A tendril of fear shot up her spine, but she forced it down. *No, don't be silly. This is Bruce.*

He turned toward the area beyond the trailers, where the university vehicles were parked together. "Your dad's property would be better."

Maggie tugged her arm free from his hold. "You want to drive all the way out there?"

"No one would interrupt us, and we could examine the dig site there together." He shifted his eyes. "I have so much to explain—" He choked on the word. "It'll take a little time."

Against her better judgement, Maggie nodded. She'd known Bruce for years. He was a friend, and she wanted to believe him.

Bruce gave a nervous laugh. "You know, I'm almost thankful this happened. It's been eating at me. I'm relieved I can explain everything to you."

A shout came from behind them, cutting him short, and they pivoted toward the voice. An undergrad raced in their direction.

"Wait up!" The young man raised his hand, frantically waving it.

"Jason?"

The boy skidded to a stop in front of Bruce. "It's Ashley." Puffing to catch his breath, he bent and grasped his knees. "There was an accident. She fell into one of the pits. Looks like she broke her arm."

"What next? Okay, I'll drive her to the hospital in Chinle. I'll be right there." He turned back to Maggie, his face tight and drawn. "We'll finish this conversation, I promise you."

She swallowed. "Yes." She raised the potsherd in her hand. "We're not done discussing this."

~

Nathan's cheeks hurt from smiling. He glanced at the clock, every second ticking down to the weekend. Sheep shearing time always brought a mix of hard work and fun, but this time, he had another reason to look forward to it—Maggie.

At a nearby desk, Yoyetewa hunched over a form, pen in hand. The rookie faced away from him, his shoulders tense, as they had been for days. Nathan stood in the doorway, one ankle crossed over the other, his shoulder leaned on the door jamb. A frisson of guilt washed through him. *Maybe I have been just a little too hard on him.*

"Hey, Yoyetewa."

Merv jumped, dropped the pen, ducked down to grab it, and smacked his head on the underside of the desk. He sprang back up, wide-eyed, clutching his head with one hand and the pen in the other. "Yes, sir?"

Nathan stifled a smile. "I need to talk to Detective Deschene about the Beaumont case. Could you grab him and meet me in conference room C?"

"Of course." Yoyetewa stood and headed out of the main workroom.

"Oh, and bring Lieutenant Benally, too."

Inside the conference room, Nathan waited mere minutes before his recruit and the two senior officers joined him.

His spine straightened on instinct when Uncle Ben walked in and sat across from him. The man didn't even bend the crease in his slacks. It was almost comical to see him beside Deschene in his wrinkled dress shirt.

Uncle Ben thumped his pen on the table, and Nathan got to the point.

"I wanted to talk about the Beaumont case, the one on the Adakai property with the looted pots."

Deschene made a quiet grunt of acknowledgement.

"Since the beginning of this case, Ms. Beaumont has been intent on … uh, assisting NNPD with the investigation." He frowned. "Every incident of violence—the attack on Terri Mitchell, Ms. Beaumont's brake lines being cut, the prowler I exchanged gunfire with—it all happened while she was staying at the mobile home. She feels she should stay there to draw out the person behind the attacks."

Nathan looked from face to face and cleared his throat. It would be helpful if Uncle Ben aka Lieutenant

Benally could give some morsel of evidence he was pleased with where this was going. Maybe just soften his expression a little. But when he was on the receiving end of that icy stare, Nathan couldn't seem to stop talking. "I don't want Ms. Beaumont in that mobile home again, so I'd like to propose an alternative plan."

Deschene sipped his coffee. "Okay. What's the plan?"

Nathan kept his eyes on the less imposing of the two men. "I think we could set up an officer in the mobile home to draw out the assailant. We could borrow one of the university's Jeeps to give the impression Ms. Beaumont is there and, when the next incident happens, we could have officers ready to engage and apprehend."

Deschene gave a slow nod. "It could work."

Nathan exhaled. "Yes, I believe it could."

"Officer Nez has a similar build, coloration. Maybe she'd be willing." Deschene turned to the lieutenant. "What do you think?"

Uncle Ben met Nathan's eyes. "I like it. Make the arrangements."

The two stood almost in sync. Deschene walked out, sipping his coffee.

Uncle Ben paused and set a hand on Nathan's shoulder. "Well done." The crow's feet at his eyes scrunched as he made an expression that could have been a smile.

Nathan relaxed. "Thanks."

Moments later, it was just him and Yoyetewa in the conference room.

The rookie practically vibrated with excitement. When Nathan turned to him, Yoyetewa spoke. "So, we're doing a stakeout? Set out the bait, wait for the bad guy, then—boom—we spring the trap?"

Nathan glanced at the clock. End of shift. "I mean, yeah. I have the next couple of days off, but you help Deschene coordinate things. You'll have to get a Jeep from the team at Canyon de Chelly." He smirked. "I suggest you take Officer Nez with you to drive it back. Don't get yourself stranded this time, huh?"

Yoyetewa's face flushed, but he smiled, and his shoulders softened. "Yes, sir."

~

As Nathan rolled down the gravel driveway in his gray king cab pickup, he couldn't hold back the smile that spread across his face.

Maggie and Jimmy stood up from the front steps of her trailer and strode out to meet Nathan as he slowed to a stop. She leaned against the lowered passenger window, dimples appearing at the corners of her heart-shaped lips. Nathan took his sweet time, savoring the sight of her, then tipped his well-worn Western hat, blocking the early morning light from his eyes.

"Why, Officer Yazzie—so, you're secretly a country boy?"

Nathan raised an eyebrow and, without looking away, turned up the volume on the radio. The voice of Willie Nelson filled the truck.

"Of course, I'm a country boy. Nothing secret about it. Most Navajo men are country boys."

A lighthearted laugh escaped her lips. She loaded Jimmy and her bag into the backseat before sliding in beside Nathan. She gave him a teasing glance. "A cool police officer listening to country music. I just wouldn't have guessed."

He turned down the radio. "Well, my family raises livestock and works acres of land. I was raised on country music. I guess I'll always relate to it." He grinned at her. "Ready to go?"

"Ready."

Nathan shifted into gear and headed toward the highway.

Maggie stretched her legs under the dashboard. "And thank you for doing this."

"Picking you up?"

Maggie shook her head. "Inviting me at all."

Nathan glanced at her again. "I told you, my mom and aunt like you. And you'll get the chance to meet my Uncle Ben. My brothers couldn't make it this year, but it'll still be a good time."

"Your mother must be so happy to have you living with her."

"Oh, I have an apartment near the station, but I spend a lot of time at my mom's. I can show you around this weekend."

"Where do your brothers live?"

"Well, Jesse works for the National Park Service and is mostly out near LeChee. Del is out near Shiprock. They're both tied up with work right now."

He straightened in his seat. "Also, I mentioned having an officer impersonate you at your dad's mobile home. We had a meeting about it yesterday. The idea went over well, so we're setting that up. Bruce is lending us one of the Jeeps for the stakeout."

A frown tugged at Maggie's lips. "You've already discussed it with Bruce? I noticed him taking a call earlier, but I thought it was about the student who injured her arm." Her frown deepened. "I waited up late last night to speak with him about a potsherd I uncovered, but... I stayed up for hours. He never came back. And that phone call... something just felt off." She turned to look out the window, brows furrowed.

As the vehicle rattled over the cattle guard onto Nathan's family's property, he saw her straighten. A small smile lifted her face.

Nathan parked his pickup behind his mother's house near a half-dozen other vehicles and opened the truck door for Maggie. He released Jimmy, grabbed her bag, and nodded toward the house. "Let's go." He shot her a grin.

The door opened into the kitchen, where his mom and Aunt Shirley stood chatting with Uncle Ben, who had his arm around Shirley's waist.

Their conversation stopped as Nathan led Maggie inside.

His mom's eyes sparkled. She walked up to Maggie, extended her arm, and gently took hold of the squash blossom necklace that hung around Maggie's neck. She spoke with stilted pronunciation. "Beautiful."

Maggie blinked rapidly. "Thank you. I'm so proud to wear this necklace."

Aunt Shirley and Uncle Ben smiled, then she tilted her head. "Is that one of John's pieces?"

Maggie swallowed. "Yes. He left it in a box of his things at the mobile home."

Aunt Shirley nodded. "He'd be happy you're wearing it."

Uncle Ben stepped forward and extended his hand. "Ya'at'eeh. I'm Nathan's uncle, Benjamin Benally.

From the Bear People Clan, born for the Deer Spring People Clan."

Maggie took his hand. "Maggie Beaumont. I'm sorry… I don't actually know my clans."

The door opened and a male voice shouted into the kitchen. "We need to get out to the shearing pens!"

Ben moved through the lemon-yellow kitchen toward the backdoor and Nathan touched Maggie's shoulder.

"We need to leave, but I'm sure my mother and aunt have something to keep you entertained. I'll see you at lunch, then we'll go out and maybe you can help shear a sheep." He hurried out the door after Uncle Ben.

Outside, Uncle Ben stopped to let Nathan catch up to him. He paused and turned to meet Nathan's eyes. "I just got a phone call. Thomas and Luke are coming to meet Maggie."

Nathan's stomach twisted. *I hope they aren't here to start trouble.*

Chapter Six

Maggie hung her purse over the back of the chair and squared her shoulders.

She breathed in the aroma of strong coffee as a percolator wheezed in the kitchen.

Wanda pointed to the table. "Sit."

Maggie immediately obeyed. Evidently, Wanda knew a few words of English, after all.

The two sisters conferred for a moment, and Shirley turned back to Maggie. "We'll start preparing the frybread, then while we wait for the dough to rest, have coffee. We've got a lot to make today to feed all these shearers."

"I'm ready when you are." She touched a hand to her heart. "I can't tell you how much I appreciate you letting me stay here and spend time with your family. It means a lot to me." Maggie nervously ran her hands down her pant legs. Cooking was never her strong suit.

A smile spread over Shirley's sun-weathered face. "You are very welcome here. We're making Navajo tacos for the shearers. Frybread filled with mutton."

"I've never had frybread, but a friend of mine tried it in town. She loved it."

"A Navajo woman needs to know how to prepare frybread. We'll show you the right way to make it—not like the bilagaànas do." Shirley shook her head in disgust.

Maggie swelled with pride. *A Navajo woman.* Suddenly, she had a new identity, and she loved it.

Maggie stood close by, observing their every move.

Shirley gave Maggie a stern look. "Use only Blue Bird flour if you want good frybread. That's very important."

Maggie nodded. These two women meant business.

Mrs. Yazzie took out two large cast-iron skillets and added several heaping spoonfuls of lard to each. She spoke to Shirley, who nodded, then translated.

"You must fry with lard. Get it smoking hot. Don't mess with that vegetable cooking oil…it isn't healthy."

Wanda went back to the table and pulled out a huge enameled dishpan and a big wooden spoon.

Shirley grabbed the kettle from the stove. "The water needs to be warm, but not too hot."

Wanda reached into the Blue Bird sack with both hands and measured out four double handfuls of flour, then three handfuls of powdered milk, a teaspoon of salt, and three heaping teaspoons of baking powder.

"Now add hot water to make a sticky dough. Knead it good," Shirley said. "Then we'll cover it with a dish towel for about twenty minutes."

While they waited, they sipped coffee and visited.

"I'd like to ask a question, if you two don't mind."

Shirley blinked. "Of course."

"I was just thinking. When I came in, you two spoke of the necklace my father made." Her hand came up to close around the chain of the squash blossom pendant. "How did my father learn to make jewelry?"

Shirley turned and spoke to Wanda, then back to Maggie. "He learned the same way that all learn the traditional crafts. It's passed down from parent to child, be it weaving or jewelry-making."

Wanda pushed to her feet and left the room quickly. Maggie's pulse jumped to her throat. *Please tell me I didn't insult her!*

Wanda returned moments later, carrying something that was clearly precious to her. She gently laid it before Maggie. Shirley translated for her sister. "She said John made this for her years ago. She wants you to see it."

It was the necklace Wanda had worn when they first met—a sterling silver and turquoise cluster design necklace—one of the most incredible things Maggie had ever seen. She flipped it over to show the artisan's name—John Adakai.

Maggie traced her thumb over the etching of his name. "It's so beautiful."

"John had a reputation for creating very fine pieces. He would often go to Santa Fe to sell his jewelry. He even had some of his work shown in a museum collection featuring traditional Dine' crafts."

Maggie beamed. "That's amazing. I'd loved to have seen that."

"They're building a new museum in Chinle. You may have the chance to see something similar soon."

Maggie's eyebrows rose. "That's great." She caressed the turquoise and looked up to meet Wanda's eyes. "Thank you for showing this to me."

"*Ahéhee'*." Shirley spoke the word slowly. "That means thank you."

Maggie repeated it, handing the necklace back to Wanda.

The sisters exchanged chuckles.

"What?" Maggie flushed.

Shirley's eyes shone with mirth. "Just... keep working on your pronunciation. *Ahéhee'.*"

When the wind-up timer rang, Wanda uncovered the dough and pinched off a portion about the size of a tennis ball. "Watch."

Maggie leaned in as Wanda shaped the ball into a disk, flattened it over her knuckles, and lowered it into the pan. The room filled with the scent of hot, savory bread. After only about twenty seconds, she poked the bubbles that rose on the bread with her fork, then flipped it to the other side. A few seconds later, the fluffy golden bread was cooling on a flattened paper bag to blot the oil.

Maggie tried her hand at the shaping and flattening. She giggled. "Not as easy as it looks." The dough split apart over her knuckles, then fell to the floor.

The older women laughed.

"Try again," Shirley said. "You'll get the hang of it."

After they'd fried a mountain of bread, they set about cutting up the toppings they'd need for the tacos.

Maggie began to relax. From the smiles she received, she felt she was passing the frybread-making lesson.

Jimmy set up a cacophony of barking in the front yard.

Maggie jumped to her feet. "I wonder what's got him so excited."

Shirley and Maggie followed Mrs. Yazzie as she made her way to the front door and opened it.

An older-model red sedan sat in the driveway. In keeping with Navajo tradition, the two visitors remained in their car until invited in. Wanda waved to the men and the car doors swung open.

Shirley gasped. "I can't believe it—it's Thomas and Luke."

"My uncle and half-brother?" Maggie asked.

"Yes. It couldn't have worked out better if we'd planned it. You'll get to meet them both now."

Maggie stayed at Wanda's heels as the pair strode to the door. Luke walked in front of a tall, older man with long, gray-streaked hair tied back in a bun.

Suddenly, Jimmy lunged from under a tree, teeth bared and ears laid back. Growling and snarling, he made straight for the two men.

Maggie flew out the door and grabbed Jimmy by his collar. "Down, boy! What's wrong with you?" She led Jimmy to the fenced-in side yard, put him behind the gate and hurried back to follow the two visitors into the kitchen. "I'm so sorry. I've never seen him react that way to anyone before."

Luke turned on Maggie. "You should keep that animal tied up!"

Thomas laid a steadying hand on Luke's shoulder, then spoke to Shirley and Wanda in their native language. He looked at Maggie. "We heard John's daughter was here."

Her heart pounded. "Yes, I'm John's daughter. I'm Maggie Beaumont."

Thomas fixed her with dark, brooding eyes. After a moment, a smile lifted the corners of his mouth. "John was my brother. I'm your Uncle Thomas."

Luke came to stand at his elbow. "She and I have already met."

Thomas quirked an eyebrow. "Oh, have you?"

She nodded. "It's true. We didn't get to talk, really, but we met." A nervous laugh escaped her. "To meet a family I didn't know existed until recently—it's a lot to take in." A lightheaded feeling overcame her, and she stumbled back when Thomas released her hand.

He grasped her arm and sat her in a chair.

Shirley gestured to the kitchen. "Yes, everyone, make yourselves comfortable. I'll get you both some coffee."

Wanda brought Maggie a glass of water. Maggie sipped it and took in the reality of her situation. She sat surrounded by people from her father's past. A kind of extended family.

"Uncle Thomas." She hesitated. "I'm sorry. Is it okay if I call you Uncle Thomas?"

He shrugged. "Sure. That's who I am." He leveled his black eyes on her again. "I can see so much of my brother in your face."

Luke bit back a laugh and rolled his eyes.

Maggie didn't know whether to smile at Thomas's compliment or frown at Luke's clear insult. She inhaled deeply and took another sip of water.

"I wanted to ask you, Uncle Thomas. I haven't had a chance to learn much about my father. Could you tell me about him? And yourself, too, of course... and my grandparents." She gave a self-conscious laugh. "I want to know everything."

Thomas dipped his head and cast a glance towards Luke. Her uncle slowly shook his head. "Okay, but you must understand, it's not customary for the Navajo to speak of the dead." He let out a breath. "Your father was my younger brother. We grew up near Olijato. There wasn't much to do, so we made our own entertainment." He shrugged. "We got into more than our share of trouble. Well, mostly me." He spooned sugar into his coffee and stirred.

"John learned to make jewelry from our father. As a boy, I didn't have enough patience to learn the craft. John had talent and made a living at it. We were close when we were younger... partners in crime. We did everything together. Then he moved to Albuquerque to get his degree and grow his jewelry business. He met your mother there, married her, and soon you were on the way."

Thomas paused, a scowl creasing his forehead. "John got involved with some Christian ministry on campus. He said he'd discovered a better way to live. He drifted away from the customs of our family and our people... rejected the old ways." Thomas's eyes blazed. "He brought Jackie here to the reservation, but your mother hated it. She left him and moved back to Albuquerque."

A deep sigh escaped Thomas's lips. "John continued to walk the Jesus Road. We fought about it often. Soon, I moved to Flagstaff and put distance between us. Before his death, we hadn't spoken for months."

"Uncle Thomas, the death certificate the lawyer showed me said he died from cirrhosis of the liver, but I thought he stopped drinking as a very young man. I don't understand how he could have had liver disease."

Wanda shook her head fiercely and said something to Shirley.

Shirley turned to Maggie. "No, he didn't have alcoholic's disease. That's a lie."

Thomas shrugged. "John did a lot of drinking when he was young. It could have done more damage than anyone realized. Or maybe he was drinking secretly."

Maggie reached out and took her uncle's sun-weathered hand and squeezed it.

She turned to look at Luke, hoping to pull him into the friendly moment, but his eyes were as hard as granite.

The laughter and warmth in the kitchen were broken by the creak of the back door. Ben stuck his head inside. "Thomas, I saw your car pull up. Come give me a hand with grilling the mutton."

"I'll be right there." He stood. "We'll talk more later. I'd best give Ben a hand with the mutton if we want to eat anytime soon."

Shirley pushed her chair back. "I guess we'd better get the rest of this outside to the table."

~

Maggie adjusted her grip on the paper plate filled with mutton, frybread, and taco fixings. She hovered by the long outdoor table set up under the brush arbor. Mrs. Yazzie had arranged the pans of food and supplies buffet-style for ease of use. Her mouth watered at the savory aromas.

But people had gathered in clumps to visit and, like a middle school cafeteria with Maggie as the new kid, she hung back uncertain of where to sit.

At the far end of the table, she spotted Uncle Thomas and Luke. She squared her shoulders and approached.

"May I join you?"

Thomas paused, a can of soda halfway to his lips. He lifted his eyes to meet hers and sat down his drink. "Yes, of course."

She settled at the table. A silence stretched between them.

"Uncle Thomas, thank you for sharing about my father earlier."

Thomas nodded. "You have no memories of your own. I can share mine."

Her smile hitched, and she tried not to fidget under their gazes. She forced her eyes up to her brother's. "The food looks great, doesn't it?"

Luke gave an awkward smile. "Yes, nothing better than a Navajo taco." He took a hearty bite, his eyes not leaving hers. "Aren't you going to do more than look at it?"

"Oh. Of course." She lifted the frybread, preparing to bite in.

"Have you tried the tacos yet?"

Maggie turned to see Nathan behind her. She smiled up at him. "Not yet. I'm just about to dig in."

"Mind if I sit next to you?"

"Of course not. Please." She patted the seat beside her.

Nathan sat, unscrewed the cap from a soda and sipped from the bottle. "I should warn you—mutton is a strong flavor. It takes a little getting used to for some people."

"Thanks for the warning." She took a nibble, closed her eyes, and gave a slow nod. The flavors and textures spread over her tongue—the soft chewy frybread, the hot and greasy mutton, the sweet fresh tomato. "I like it. It *is* different, but I like it." She pulled her face into a mock-serious expression, and nodded slowly. "You know, you're right. I taste the sage flavor …I'd say it's the sage from your north pasture, for sure."

Nathan laughed out loud. "No, this is definitely east pasture sage you're tasting."

He bit into his taco, held up a finger, then pointed to it. "You made this? It's great."

Maggie's cheeks warmed. "No, no, your mother and aunt did most of it. They just let me help a little."

Nathan repeated, "It's great. You're being modest."

Maggie shook her head. "Believe me, I'm not."

She gestured to Thomas. "Uncle Thomas was just offering to tell me more about when he and my dad were young."

"Oh, that's good. I'm glad he's able to fill you in with more of their old stories."

Maggie turned to Thomas again. "So, Uncle Thomas, you were saying earlier that even though my dad walked the Jesus Road, you are very traditional. And that led to a break between you and him. He left behind some letters I've been reading, and he mentions in one of them that you two clashed over the difference in your beliefs." Her lips turned down in a frown. "Could you explain that to me?" Her eyes darted to Luke. "Maybe it's because I didn't grow up with siblings, but I find it hard to understand."

Thomas sighed and laid his taco on his plate. "Yes. John and I grew up traditionally." Thomas's face hardened, and he stared past her into space, his eyes blazing. "The idea that my brother would choose to leave our traditions behind to chase white men's beliefs and—" His lip curled back from his teeth. He focused on her face again. "You need to understand. While you're half-white, you're also half-Navajo. You need to know the history of our people—the things we've had to endure."

Nathan nodded. "I told her a little. The BIA schools…"

But Maggie's eyes locked onto Thomas' face, drinking in every word the man spoke.

Thomas rested his hands next to his plate and curled them into fists. "Yes. The schools and so many other things just within my lifetime."

He raised his head and his eyes bored into Maggie's. "Let me tell you another story. When John and I were boys, there was a carnival that came to Olijato. Rides, games, music. It drew big crowds. I guess I was about nine years old, and John was about six. We were outside playing near the road. A car filled with white men drove by with its windows down, heading to the fairground. The car slowed, and one man leaned out the window and shouted to us, telling us to come to the carnival and there'd be free popcorn.

"Later after dinner, John kept asking to go to the fair. We had no money for games or rides, no money to shop at the stalls. Still, my little brother wanted free popcorn and to hear the music. I talked our mother into letting us go.

"We rode a horse to the fairground. A band was playing on a nearby stage." His eyes lit up for a moment at the memory. "John was so excited. He ran ahead of me. He'd seen the white man from the car. I arrived just in time to hear John ask about the popcorn."

Thomas's face turned to granite. "I still remember it all. I remember exactly what the man said. He pointed to a big, dirty trash can and said, 'There's the free Injun popcorn right there.'" Thomas' eyes burned into Maggie's as if trying to brand his words into her soul.

"He and his friends laughed and walked away. My little brother cried all the way home." Thomas opened his fists, and Maggie could see the imprints his fingernails had made in his palms. His voice became low and dangerous. "And this is the path John chose to emulate. This is the people whose footsteps he followed. He may have forgotten the little boy crying at the fair, but I never can."

Maggie's heart sank as a wave of sorrow washed over her, leaving her grief-stricken. She didn't know when she'd ever seen someone so poisoned by life as Thomas. The things he'd lived through had embittered him. Then she looked at Luke, who sat silently listening to the story.

She put her hands over her eyes, trying to block out the image of her young father and uncle being treated like nothing more than stray dogs. She reached out and touched her uncle's hand. "Oh, Uncle Thomas. I'm so sorry."

Thomas inhaled a deep breath and let it out slowly. "Well...you wanted to know why we disagreed. Now you have your answer."

~

Maggie carried an armload of dirty dishes into Wanda's kitchen and set them into the deep farmhouse sink. Wanda followed with leftovers and began wrapping them for the refrigerator.

The kitchen door swung open, and Luke plodded in, still wearing the same angry, hangdog expression he'd worn all day. He dropped into a chair at the table and leveled his gaze at her.

Wanda exited the house again to continue her lunch cleanup.

A tense silence filled the air between Maggie and Luke.

"Is there something you wanted, Luke? Could I get you another soda?" She searched his face, hoping to find his stony expression replaced by a more welcoming one.

"No thanks. I'm fine."

Maggie sat down with him, drew in a breath, and tapped her fingers on the table. "Luke, I hope we can be friends. I mean, we are family. I know we didn't grow up together, but I love the thought of having a brother—someone out there I share a parent with." She slid her hand toward him across the table. "Maybe in time we can become closer."

He dropped his hands into his lap. "Family based on what? The fact that my dad sired you twenty-something years ago, and then your mother abandoned him before you were even born? And then, out of some misguided sense of duty, or maybe fantasy about the little girl he never got to raise, he put you on a pedestal and left you the few possessions he had in life." Luke latched his eyes onto the silver and turquoise necklace she wore. "Yeah. The special, half-white daughter he never knew got all his affection and the last works of his hands. The son he left behind—forgotten."

"Luke, I'm so sorry. If only I knew how to make things better." She pulled the necklace over her head and held it out to him. "Please take it. I want you to have it. I'd like to share everything he left with you."

His face softened for a moment, and he took the necklace from her. He rubbed his thumbs over the turquoise stones and clutched it in his hand. "Thanks, sister." Luke stood up, the necklace in his fist. He turned his gaze on her, his stare hardening, transforming before her eyes. Then he threw the necklace. It hit the table with a hard *thunk*, skidding off the edge into the floor. His eyes blazed with anger. "But no thanks."

Luke turned and stormed out the back door, slamming it behind him.

Maggie sat in stunned silence, scalding tears streaming down her face. She folded her arms on the table and rested her head on them, her shoulders shuddering as she wept.

~

Nathan stepped into the kitchen to see Maggie at his mother's table, swiping tears from her face. He sped across the room and knelt beside her. "Maggie, what in the world happened? Luke stormed outside like he wanted to punch someone. He said something to Thomas, got into the car and drove off, barely saying goodbye. Did you two argue?"

She grabbed a napkin and dabbed her eyes. "He hates me. I mean, he truly hates me, and there's nothing I can do to make it better." She wiped her nose. "I'll just have to accept that fact."

Nathan squeezed her shoulder. "Come on. Let's go for a little walk. You need some fresh air." He reached down and picked up the squash-blossom necklace. "Man, that guy's got a temper, doesn't he?"

Nathan took Maggie by her wrist and led her out the front door and around the side of the house. "Come on. I want to show you the hogan my brothers and I built."

Maggie's face lit up. "I would love to see the inside."

"Well, there isn't a lot to see, but it's where we lived for most of my early life."

As they circled the house, the hogan came into view, the Lukachukais in the distance behind the domed, earthen structure. The savory aroma of roasting mutton still lingered on the breeze, along with the ever-present scent of sage and juniper.

Nathan pulled open the door of the hogan and led Maggie inside. He took a deep breath, inhaling the earthy scent. "On a hogan, the door always faces east to welcome the rising sun and the sacred white mountain."

Inside, the walls consisted of wooden poles chinked with mud. In the center of the room stood the wood-burning stove where his mother had prepared countless meals, the pipe exiting through a smoke hole in the ceiling. Under their feet, packed dirt made up the floor.

"Did your father live here too, Nathan?"

Sadness passed over his eyes. "No. My dad died in a car accident when I was ten years old. A drunk driver ran a stop sign and broad-sided my dad's car. We lived with some relatives for a while, then my brothers and I built this hogan."

Nathan stuffed his hands into his pockets and looked wistfully around the one-room dwelling. "Not much in here now."

"Well, there's this." Maggie crossed to an old weaving loom on the far side of the room.

"Oh, yeah." He came to stand beside her, running a hand over the time-worn wood. "This was my great-grandmother's. She wove a lot of beautiful rugs on it." He gave a soft laugh. "She literally used it to death."

"It's hard to believe four people used to live in this place." He turned and walked to an old table and chair. "But we did, and we were happy."

"I believe you. It's the love, trust and sense of family that makes one happy, not the things they possess."

Nathan stepped close to her and draped the necklace around her neck again. He cupped her cheeks. "What about you, Maggie? Did you have those things growing up? And what about now? Do you think you could leave the big city and live a simple life without all the fancy trappings?"

Her hand came to rest against his. A smile lifted the corners of her lips. "You might not believe me, but I feel much more at home here on the reservation than I ever did in the city. I sometimes think I'm better suited to a simpler life."

He ran his fingers down her cheek and leaned in close. "Well, one thing's for sure—the simple life looks beautiful on you." His gaze drifted to her lips.

Footsteps crunched outside the door. A moment later, Ben appeared, his silhouette cutting into the dim light of the hogan.

"Nathan, Maggie." Ben glanced at them. "Do you know why Thomas and Luke tore out of here? It upset your aunt."

Maggie clenched her hands. "Luke was upset with me. That's why."

Ben paused. "Oh." He took a step toward the door. "Well, that's all I needed to know." He met Nathan's eyes, glanced to Maggie, and left again without another word.

Maggie's mouth twitched upwards. "He really rules the roost, doesn't he?"

Nathan shrugged. "He's the boss, for sure. Whether at the station or at home. He's good at it, though."

"Oh, he's your boss at work, too? That must be awkward."

Nathan shook his head. "No. Uncle Ben doesn't treat me any differently than anyone else at the station. He has high expectations, though." Nathan shot her a wry smile. "To be honest, I live in fear of the day I disappoint him."

Maggie set a hand on his shoulder. "You won't. I don't see how you could ever disappoint anyone."

Nathan gave her a warm smile. "Okay... let's find something else to get your mind off your angry half-brother. Did you bring your gun with you today?"

"Yes! It's in my purse. Are you going to teach me how to stay out of doorways while people are shooting at me?"

"That was the plan. At least part of it." He lifted an eyebrow.

Surprise and suspicion swept over her face. "Hmm... okay. Well, let's do it, then."

He led her out of the cool, earthen structure and back into the hot, dry air. "Let's go over in the trees where we'll have a bit of shade."

Nathan directed her into a small copse of pine trees beyond the hogan. She looked up at him, nervousness, even shyness filled her eyes. Where was the self-confident woman who'd thought she could fend off would-be murderers single-handedly?

She took her Ruger from her purse and held it down at her side.

"Let's have a look at that." Nathan took it from her, ejected the clip, and then re-inserted it.

"Ruger, that's a pretty good gun."

He took a stance behind her and wrapped his arms around her, raising her hands to shoulder level. "Just remember—shooting at a moving man is much different than a stationary target."

"Of course."

He nuzzled close to her ear. "Shoulders relaxed.

Breath steady. Don't fight the recoil."

Her hands didn't shake as he guided her aim toward a soda can sitting on a stump. The air fell quiet, as if the trees held their breath.

"Whenever you're ready," Nathan murmured.

Maggie didn't hesitate. She squeezed the trigger, and the shot cracked through the pines. The can flipped off the stump, spinning through the air before clattering to the ground.

Nathan blinked. "Wow."

She turned to look at him, a sly smile tugging at her lips. "You expected me to miss?"

He grinned, pride and surprise mixing in his chest. "I didn't say that."

"Nathan! You out here?"

Nathan turned to see Uncle Ben trudging toward them. "I need you to help with the sheep."

Nathan sighed, glancing back at Maggie. "Be right there." He shot her a look, half apology, half admiration. "Sorry. We'll do this again soon."

Nathan shook his head, following his uncle toward the pasture, but he couldn't stop the small smile that lingered on his face.

Chapter Seven

In no hurry to return to the kitchen after her visit to the hogan, Maggie spent the rest of the evening on the stoop out front, visiting with Wanda and Shirley.

Maggie closed her eyes against the last purple rays of sunset that hovered above the horizon. The warm colors illuminated low, flat clouds that rolled towards her. The temperature had dropped, and a pleasant breeze picked up.

Nathan's family's home was inviting. The house itself was small and unimposing, but it exuded hominess and love. *Could I live here, live this way so separated from the bustling world I grew up in?* Though her heart yearned for it, many challenges stood in her way. Still, with every day that passed, an irresistible force pulled her to Nathan.

Nathan himself was pretty great.

A formidable protector, kind, and smart. Maggie couldn't imagine why anyone wouldn't find him amazing. A man of conviction and honor. But her heart twisted painfully when she thought about the truth that lay between them. In the hogan, they'd stood so close that they shared a breath. If Nathan's Uncle Ben hadn't interrupted, he'd have kissed her—she knew it. And part of her had longed for it.

But she couldn't let that happen. Giving her heart to a man investigating her father—who suspected him of stealing the artifacts from the shed—felt impossible. Trusting Nathan completely would never come easy. Not when he believed her family capable of such betrayal. Maggie shook her head. No, that couldn't happen.

Wanda touched Maggie's arm and pulled her from her daydream. She pointed to the distant clouds.

Beside her, Shirley's voice was flat. "A storm is coming."

~

The sound of a car's engine reverberating snapped her from her reverie. It skidded to a stop just feet from where Maggie sat. Merv jumped out.

She shot to her feet, her nerves tingling. "What's wrong?"

Wide eyed, he scanned his surroundings. "Where are Sergeant Yazzie and Lieutenant Benally? They need to get to your mobile home now. Sarah Nez has been shot."

"No!" The word choked from her throat. Guilt churned in her stomach. *Someone shot Sarah Nez because they believed she was me.*

"How badly is she hurt?"

He shook his head. "I don't know yet. But I need to speak with Sergeant Yazzie right now."

She turned to look at the fields spreading beyond the small house. "He's somewhere out in the pastures, helping shear the sheep. I'm not sure exactly where. There's so much land..." She led Merv through the side yard to the back of the house.

Wanda and Nathan stood working under the brush arbor. Maggie and Merv raced to them.

Merv locked eyes with Nathan. "Sergeant, do you know where Lieutenant Benally is? Sarah Nez was just wounded at the Adakai property."

Nathan paled and turned to his mother. After a quick exchange, Nathan shook his head. He looked to Maggie and then Merv. "No, he could be in one of a few places. Tell me what happened with Nez."

"She had changed clothes and was outside unloading groceries from the Jeep." Merv grimaced. "The shooter was waiting. She was hit in the chest. Deschene called for EMS and then sent me to find you and Lieutenant Benally."

Nathan extended his open palm. "Yoyetewa, go find the lieutenant. Go with him as soon as you find him. I'll take the cruiser and get to the scene."

Merv nodded and handed over the keys, following Wanda as she headed across the yard, speaking quickly in Dine'.

Nathan dashed for the cruiser.

Maggie ran to keep up, leaning into the window as he closed the door. "I want to go with you."

His eyes widened. "What? No. There's been a shooting there."

"Exactly. They think they got me, and the place is crawling with cops. No way is the shooter still there." Her hands clenched over the top of the door. "Please. It's my fault this happened to Officer Nez. I need to see with my own eyes that she's okay. You know?"

"Oh, no. I…" He shook his head. "Alright. Get in."

Maggie didn't hesitate. She scrambled into the passenger seat, barely clicking her seatbelt before he sped down the driveway.

She rolled down the window part way, the wind whipping her hair around her face. Thunder rumbled in the distance. "I just can't believe this happened to Nez. I hope she'll be okay."

"Guess we won't know 'til she gets to the hospital."

Maggie hung her head and shook it slowly. "Why did I ever agree to this? What if she dies because of me?"

Nathan turned to her for a moment, his face stern. "Look, Maggie. There's something you need to understand. Police officers sign up for this kind of thing. We know what we're getting into and what the risks are. A cop puts on their uniform and willingly walks into danger. We do it to protect our communities…our people." Lightning flashed and illuminated the strong lines of his face. "Don't you feel guilty about anything. Sarah Nez is a police officer because she wants to be. You can feel grateful, but don't feel guilty." His hand left the wheel and reached over to squeeze hers.

Understanding flooded Maggie, and she nodded. "Yes, I see what you mean. Thank you for explaining that to me."

He smiled at her and turned onto the highway, the car's headlights cutting through the growing darkness that settled over the rolling desert.

Maggie's fingers traced the outline of the concealed gun pocket in her crossbody purse. Nathan had promised another gun safety lesson, but now everything was uncertain. Would she even stay at his mother's house tonight?

She wrapped a hand around the chain of her squash blossom necklace, then removed it and put it away in her purse.

The scream of an ambulance shattered her thoughts. Nathan pulled over to let it pass, then got back up to speed. "That'd be Nez," he muttered, his voice cracking despite the false calm he tried to maintain.

A black SUV tailed the ambulance.

"Yeah. I, uh, guess I won't be able to see her after all." Maggie blinked back tears. Sarah Nez had made her own decisions, still guilt gnawed at Maggie's insides

A sharp mental image burned behind her eyes. The gravel yard in front of her father's mobile home, the ground soaked with blood. A woman who looked similar to Maggie sprawled in the growing pool of red, eyes wide, gasping, a ragged hole in her chest.

Though she'd never done it before, Maggie sent up a prayer for Sarah Nez.

She switched on the cabin light, dug tissues out of her purse, and dabbed at her eyes. They sat in silence for a moment as rain began to patter on the roof of the cruiser.

Headlights in the rearview mirror blinded her. "Does that idiot have his brights on?" She turned and looked out the back window but couldn't make out what kind of vehicle followed them. "Who would tailgate a police vehicle like that?"

Suddenly, the cruiser jolted. Metal screamed as they were rammed from behind.

Nathan growled, fighting to control the vehicle.

Another bump, and the cruiser careened into a gulley with a sickening crunch.

Maggie froze. A shotgun blast broke the air and the back window.

Nathan grabbed her wrist. "Get out of the car!"

He shoved the door open and dragged Maggie behind him. Crouched behind the cruiser, he drew his Glock.

Maggie pulled her Ruger from her purse. Every word of Nathan's lecture about how she'd used her gun incorrectly ran through her brain. She'd do it right this time.

Rain soaked her clothing. A streak of lightning split the sky, illuminating the surrounding terrain.

"Okay, get ready, Maggie. We're gonna run hard for the dense brush. When we get there, you stay low."

She took a deep breath and nodded. "Ready when you are."

He swiped a sleeve across his face, scanned his surroundings, and then nodded. "Run for those bushes!"

Her heart pounded with adrenaline as she and Nathan bolted for the cover of brush. Soon footsteps hammered close behind them.

They plastered themselves behind an outcropping of rocks, gravel crunching ominously nearby.

Maggie swallowed, her heart in her throat. With a slow exhale, she removed the safety from her gun. She

peeked around the rock, careful to stay behind cover—
no standing in open doorways this time.

A hooded figure emerged from the thicket, rain
dripping like ink from his black clothes. A flash of
lightning revealed something metallic in his hand.

A muzzle flash from the shooter's gun, and Nathan
spun around and hit the ground.

"Nathan!"

"Run, Maggie—run for cover."

As if shot from a cannon, she leapt to her feet and
ran toward a stand of pinyon bushes. Her feet sank into
the wet, sandy earth, slowing her stride.

A shot rang past her, and she willed herself to
push harder. Finally, she reached the pinyon bushes,
and all but flew into them, sliding through brush, sand,
and rocks. Her shirt ripped, the left sleeve nearly
tearing off. Fire shot down her arm as the flesh scraped
away. She raised her gun with both hands and shot at
the hooded figure.

The sound of her pursuer's footsteps stopped.
Another shot whizzed past her.

"Please, God. Help us."

From where Nathan had fallen, a muzzle flashed in
the darkness. Nathan was still in the fight.

Lightning streaked again. The figure came toward
her and raised his gun. She lifted herself to her knees
and gripped her Ruger in both hands, arms extended.
She pulled the trigger.

The figure in black grunted and fell to the ground,
then immediately stood and charged her again.

Bright lights cut through the darkness, and an
approaching engine roared.

The shooter turned and fled to his SUV. She heard the vehicle's door slam. The engine roared to life, then screeched into the night.

Maggie flipped her Ruger's safety on, then shielded her eyes against the oncoming headlights.

A dark-colored pickup pulled to the side of the road. A door opened, then slammed.

"Maggie? Sarge?"

Relief surged through her. "Merv!"

Seeing his figure step in front of his headlights, Maggie ran up to the vehicle.

Loud footsteps approached them, splashing through the wet sand. Maggie whirled around and raised her gun. Her eyes locked with Nathan's as he stood before her, his hands raised in a nonthreatening stance, then winced and rolled his shoulder. "Whoa, easy, Maggie, it's just me."

"Sorry." She put her Ruger back in her purse, annoyed to notice her hands trembling. She grabbed him by both arms and drew closer. A gash across the upper arm of his shirt steadily darkened as he bled. "Oh, Nathan! You're hurt."

He gave a quick smile and clamped a hand over the injury. "Just a graze."

The driver's window rolled down and Lieutenant Benally's voice barked. "Get in."

They separated, and Maggie slid into the back, Nathan beside her, with Merv taking the front passenger seat.

Nathan wrapped a protective arm around her shoulder, and a calm washed over her. The rhythmic swiping of the windshield wipers and hushed voices of the men speaking softly lulled her into a state of serenity.

The abrupt silence when Benally turned off the engine snapped Maggie back to the present.

Ben left the keys in the pickup and turned to look at them. "I'm going to join the search for the assailant. Yoyetewa, you get these two to the hospital. Nathan, after you get patched up, coordinate with the detail guarding Nez. Make sure no one without clearance gets near her. I'll get a ride home with another unit."

Nathan nodded. "Of course."

Fire surged down the raw skin of Maggie's left arm. Her head felt light, and she closed her eyes. With Nathan taking charge, she could finally rest.

~

Nathan led them through the ER's sliding doors and to the check-in desk. Merv took command, shouting to the triage nurse. "We've got a wounded officer. He needs to be seen now!"

A heartbeat later, the nurse led Nathan into an exam room, Maggie pushed along in his shadow.

After getting his arm cleaned and bandaged, Nathan left the exam room and glimpsed Officers Tsosie and Kee standing in the hallway beyond. Nez's guard detail.

Nathan spoke with Leslie Tsosie, who updated him—Nez was out of surgery. She was in critical but stable condition.

A familiar voice filtered through to him. "I'm here to check on Maggie Beaumont. I was told she was hurt and coming in here."

Nathan spun as he recognized the voice coming from beyond the doors. "Bruce Adams."

"And I need to speak to the police officer she came in with."

Nathan pushed through the doors and strode to the desk.

Bruce looked like he hadn't slept in a week. His curly hair was a tumbleweed, and his pale skin made the shadows under his eyes raccoon-like.

He took a step toward Nathan. "Officer—"

Nathan looked to the nurse behind the desk. "Is there a room where we can talk?"

She directed them to a private sitting room where he and Bruce sat on opposite sides of a flimsy conference table. Nathan folded his hands in front of himself and fixed Bruce with a flat look. "Well, you said you needed to speak with me."

~

An hour later, Nathan escorted Bruce Adams into the Chinle station, his wrists cuffed. He led him to an interrogation room and secured him.

Detective Deschene met Nathan at the door. "When you called, you said to meet you here. What is going on?"

"Bruce Adams just confessed to digging up Anasazi artifacts at the Adakai property. Lieutenant Benally and an FBI agent will be here shortly. Everyone will get the details then."

An hour later, Nathan stood, arms folded, in the corner of the interrogation room. The FBI agent tapped for the case, Elise Martin, sat across from Bruce

Adams, watching silently with cat-like patience. Detective Deschene, beside her, leaned down and got in Bruce's face.

"So, you expect me to believe you were digging up ancient Anasazi artifacts on the Adakai property and were clueless about what was really going on? Then Maggie Beaumont showed up at the mobile home on the land and spoiled your plan to dig up a fortune in pots and artifacts."

Bruce put his hands over his face and shook his head forcefully. "No! I'm telling you—that's not how it was."

Nathan bolted out of the corner and slammed his hand on the table. "I've heard enough of your fairy tales. A few days ago, we asked you to come in and examine the artifacts we'd found in the shed on Maggie's property. You lied about their origin and dates. Maggie's come close to dying several times. I want to hear the truth from you. Now!"

Bruce's face distorted with fear. "Sergeant Yazzie, I'm trying to tell you the truth." He sucked in a ragged breath and started again. "I got an anonymous phone call when we first received the go-ahead to excavate at Canyon de Chelly. Some guy saying he'd make it worth my while if I also dug on the Adakai property. That he'd found some relics he believed to be ancient Zuni. He said it was on a piece of land with an old mobile home where the owner had died." Bruce shook his head, his voice choked. "My son had a rare blood disorder, and the debt was killing me... It sounded so easy. I never dreamed anyone would get hurt.

"So, I went out there a couple of times and started digging on my time off. Sure enough, I found twelfth-century Anasazi relics. I started leaving things in that old storage shed behind the mobile home for the guy to pick up. He'd leave a nice stack of cash for me."

"Well, imagine my shock when I discovered Maggie is actually the new owner of that place. I couldn't believe it! Soon, I got another of the anonymous calls telling me to get Maggie off the property—he didn't care how I did it. I refused. I told him I was done with the whole deal."

He looked from face to face. "You must understand. I think the world of Maggie. I'd never do anything to hurt her." Bruce's hollow eyes burned into Nathan's.

I hate to admit it, but I think he's telling the truth.

Detective Deschene sat on the edge of his desk. "And you have no idea who this so-called anonymous caller was?"

Bruce hung his head. "No, I don't know who it was. But the guy sounded real young, and now there's somebody suddenly finding excuses to be around Maggie and the mobile home." He looked up at Nathan. "The guy really gives me the creeps. I can't prove it, but I'd bet anything it was Luke Adakai."

~

The next morning, Nathan strode down the white-on-white halls of the hospital. His eyes locked onto the partially open door of Maggie's room.

Maggie's voice filtered down the hall. "Zinnias! How did you know these are my favorites?"

The voice that answered was higher, brighter. Terri Mitchell. "Oh, I know you always go for the most colorful things, so I must have made a good guess."

"I guess you know me pretty well."

Terri's tone flattened. "I can't believe the things that have happened since we've been here. I'm so grateful you're okay." A pause. "I got a phone call from the head of our department last night. They're sending out a replacement for Bruce first thing tomorrow. We'll have to get him oriented and settled in. The whole thing boggles my brain."

"What do you mean?"

Nathan's conscience twinged at unintentionally eavesdropping. He lengthened his stride.

"I'll, uh, tell you on the drive back."

Nathan reached the door and tugged it open. He peeked around the doorframe and shot Maggie a smile.

"Come in, Nathan. Terri's here, too, but I can visit with both of you."

He hesitantly made his way to her bedside, rubbing the back of his neck. "Sorry to interrupt. I'll only stay a minute." He turned to Terri. "How are you, Ms. Mitchell?"

A friendly smile lit her face. "I'm doing well, Officer Yazzie. Thanks for asking."

He pulled up a chair and sat down. "Maggie, I know the doctor's releasing you today. I hope you'll come back to my mom's place until this is over with. You'll be safe there."

Maggie hung her head. "Thank you, Nathan, but I really need to spend at least one night at Canyon de Chelly. Terri told me we're getting a replacement for

Bruce tomorrow. I think I should be there to help him settle in."

"What about that arm of yours? How will you work with that injury?" Nathan scrunched his face as he caught sight of her painful-looking arm.

"Very carefully." She snickered. "Okay, not funny. But I have a few things I want to take care of in my trailer." She looked at Terri and winked. "I'll put my gun under my pillow."

Nathan bolted upright. "Oh, no you don't! Give me that gun."

Maggie and Terri both laughed out loud.

"Seriously, I'll be okay for one night, then I'll go to your mom's at the end of the workday. Oh, how is Jimmy doing? I hope your mother isn't upset that I left him at her place."

"Of course not. Jimmy's fitting in just fine, but I know he'll be happy to see you."

"Thank you, Nathan. And please thank your mother for me."

"Okay, I'm not happy about this. But promise me you'll come to my mother's tomorrow afternoon. I'll stay there, too. That'll make two police officers on the place to protect you."

"I will. I promise."

~

Across the large workroom, Nathan saw Detective Deschene leaning over his desk with Lieutenant Benally and FBI Agent Martin. He crossed to join them, hearing the agent's light voice as he approached.

"I can't help but wonder if Bruce Adams has more information than he's telling."

Deschene shot her down, voice calm. "He came forward to offer information, incriminated himself. Set himself up for jail time and fines—probably ruined his career. He's told us what he knows."

Nathan stood at his uncle's elbow. "Discussing the Beaumont case?"

Benally nodded. "It's good you're here. I wanted to ask you something."

With his heart in his throat, Nathan struggled to swallow around it. The weight of three sets of eyes pinned him in place. "Of course."

"This case deals with the looting of tribal artifacts, rare Anasazi objects. Bruce Adams excavated them from the Adakai property. His associate, Maggie Beaumont, inherited the lease on the land. The operation started after the previous owner died. These artifacts were left on her property to be presumably sold." Benally tilted his head and met Nathan's eyes. "Why haven't you looked into Ms. Beaumont as a suspect in the looting?"

A rushing filled Nathan's ears. "What? Someone's been trying to kill Maggie! Why would we suspect her?"

"Which could have nothing to do with the looting. When her friend, Bruce Adams, was arrested, he pointedly drew attention away from Ms. Beaumont." Benally's stare was flat. "But you've spent time with her, invited her to stay with your family, and call her by first name. Have you become too close for this case?"

"No, and even Detective Deschene says Bruce had no reason to lie."

Benally stood silent for a long moment. "I'm not saying that Ms. Beaumont is behind the looting. I don't think it's very likely. The attempts on her life are probably connected. I'm asking why you haven't considered it."

Nathan froze. Why hadn't he considered it? Had a pretty face thrown off his investigative instincts?

No. He could feel in his bones that Maggie was innocent.

"Instinct. I know enough about Ms. Beaumont to know that would be out of character for her."

Benally's face tightened. "I hope you're right."

Nathan turned to the desk, to the document Deschene and Martin still leaned over. "We should listen to Bruce Adams, look into Luke Adakai."

The woman straightened and flipped a tendril of red hair over her shoulder. "Twenty-two years old, born on the reservation to John Adakai and Anne Begay. He works at the trading post."

Nathan nodded. "Yeah. But he spent summers on his father's property. He may have discovered the artifacts and started the dig, expecting the lease to transfer to him."

Deschene looked at the paper, a transcript of Bruce Adams' testimony. "Adams claimed the voice on the phone was a young guy. Could have been Luke Adakai."

Nathan gestured to the paper. "If it was him, he'd be looking at years in jail, thousands of dollars of fines. That might be worth killing his own sister to keep quiet."

Martin raised a hand to her lips. "And that led to the murder attempt on Sarah Nez."

Beside him, Benally snatched the paper from Deschene's hands and threw it on the table. All eyes turned to him. "This is all speculation." He locked eyes with each of them. "What we need is evidence."

Chapter Eight

Maggie and Terri pulled up at the Canyon de Chelly campsite. Maggie got out of the Jeep and turned a slow circle, taking in the collection of trailers and tables. Everything was the same but felt different.

The news about Bruce's betrayal had shocked more than just her. A hollow haze permeated the site. A collection of undergrads sat silently at one of the outside tables, their coffee growing cold in front of them. Ashley and Jason stood under a canopy, speaking in subdued voices.

Maggie shook her head and started toward her trailer. Terri took her by the arm. "What?"

"I think I'd like to be alone for a bit. I'm just... tired. Maybe I'll nap." *Though I don't know if I could sleep after the news about Bruce.*

Terri hesitated at the steps. "Okay. I'll come by after a bit and pick you up for dinner."

"Yeah. See you then." She pasted a smile on for Terri, then let it drop as she left.

Maggie pulled the door closed and flipped on the lights. Same trailer, same bed and boxes, same dog bowls. *I really miss Jimmy right now.*

She settled into an armchair, wrapping a blanket around her. Staring ahead, she caught sight of the box of her father's belongings.

Pulling it close, she grabbed the bundle of letters. *These should distract me for a while.*

After reading most of them, Maggie felt she knew her father better. His kindness, warmth, and care all radiated through his words. She noticed the lack of letters around the time he remarried, how they became fewer as the years went on. There were only a few left. She clutched the fourth-to-last, burying her face against the paper, the vellichor comforting.

December 19, 2023
Dear Jackie,
This time of year always makes me think of family. I hope you and Margaret are happy and well.

I know that my attempts to reach out never land. I guess by this point, I've accepted it. Still, I pray for you two. That you are healthy and enjoying yourselves.

Christmastime brings that out in me. Maybe makes me sentimental. Luke came to visit me today, though Anne wouldn't. We mostly sat quietly and watched It's a Wonderful Life. *I haven't been feeling well—nausea and pain in my abdomen—and he made me some tea. He surprises me sometimes.*

I am so tired lately, my age catching up to me, I suppose. It makes me reflect on all the years. I have many fond memories, many of them about you, Jackie.

Do you remember our wedding? I sure do.

That was one of those rare, perfect days. I remember the cold air snapping at my heels all the way to the judge, tugging at the borrowed suit where the cuffs were too short. The building was so grand, impressive. The best part was walking in to see you in that little white dress, your mother's pearls around your neck. You must have been freezing, but the smile you gave me warmed the entire room.

Jack and Kelly from our macroeconomics class were the witnesses. Do you ever talk to them anymore? They sent me a Christmas card. They moved to Gallup last year.

I remember you gave me such a hard time for running late, but that's what growing up on the rez does, I guess. I just remember your hand in mine after we signed the license, the warmth of your skin, the smell of orange blossoms from your perfume.

It was snowing as we left and the flakes stuck in your hair as we ran for the taxi. You looked like an angel.

They say that there is one perfect person, the one that got away. I think you were mine.

Merry Christmas, Jackie.

Love,

John

~

The paper crumpled under Maggie's shaking hands. Her eyes blurred, and she set it back in the box. *And she never even read these words.*

Maggie snatched up her phone and typed in her mother's number.

Her blood boiled as she waited for one ring, two.

"Maggie, honey, I was wondering when you'd call—"

"Mom." Her voice sounded low, ragged to her own ears.

A pause. "Is everything okay? You sound upset."

Maggie remained silent.

"I guess you're still in Arizona on that dig you were so excited about."

"Yes, I'm in Arizona. I've been spending time at my dad's place. You know... my dad, John Adakai."

Silence stretched between them. "Maggie, your father—"

Maggie cut her off. "He's dead. He died a few weeks ago."

A gasp came through the phone. "John is dead?"

Maggie sniffed and wiped her nose. "Yes, he's dead. Mom, how could you? How could you lie to me for twenty-five years? How could you hide the fact that I had a Navajo father and deny me the opportunity to know him?" She choked on the words. "What a horrible thing to do."

"Oh, I've got to sit down." Jackie released a heavy sigh. "Maggie, I've dreaded this day. I don't even know where to begin."

"Twenty-five years, Mother." She screamed. "Were you ever going to tell me the truth?"

"I wanted to. So many times."

"Mother, all these beautiful letters he wrote you. He loved you. He wanted me... wanted us. Wanted us to be a family. How could you marry him, then turn around and abandon him?"

"I never meant for things to happen that way. I did love John. I adored him. But, honey, I couldn't adjust to life on that reservation. We'd just graduated, and both had wonderful opportunities ahead. There was absolutely no future for us on the reservation."

She paused. "John became a Christian, and suddenly that was the number one priority in his life. He felt he had a mission—something he was called to do among the Navajo. He wanted to create his jewelry and evangelize his people." Another deep sigh. "I... I wasn't cut out for it. At first, I begged him to move to Albuquerque with me, but he refused. I loved him, but there was no hope for us. I just gave up and ended the marriage."

"But why did you refuse him a relationship with me? That seems cruel and punitive."

"I didn't mean to, honey. When you were born, I wasn't going to send my newborn baby to visit in another state. Then I met Darrell, and he accepted you with open arms. Everything with John just fell apart."

"Mother, I don't know if I can ever forgive you for this." Maggie felt rage rise in her throat. She screamed into the phone. "Don't you understand what you denied me? You changed the course of my entire life!" She heaved a ragged breath. "I can't talk right now. I have to go. Goodbye, Mom."

"Maggie..."

She swiped her phone off and threw it down on the bed.

She sat in the dim quiet of the trailer, the phone screen black. Her hands still trembled, not from cold, but from the echo of her mother's voice—twenty-five years of silence cracking open like a thunderstorm over a lonely mesa, fierce and unrelenting.

~

Maggie's phone buzzed. She picked it up and saw Nathan's named illuminated on the screen. *I just can't right now.*

She sent the call to voicemail.

A knock sounded at her door. Maggie threw aside her afghan and sat up in bed. *I wish people would leave me alone.*

She pulled the door open to find a cheerful Terri standing on the stoop. The smile slid from her face. "Wow, Mags. You look rough."

Maggie nodded. "Yeah, I believe you, but at the moment, I guess I don't much care." She stepped back and waved Terri in.

"Is this about Bruce?"

A short laugh burst from Maggie's mouth. "Bruce? Yeah, him too."

"Too?"

"And my mother." She collapsed into a chair. "I read some more of my dad's letters. I was so furious with my mom that I called her." Maggie swiped her hair behind her ear. "We really had it out."

Terri's blue eyes widened. "Oh, hon. You have had a day." She knelt beside the chair and put her arms around her. "You feel up to eating dinner?"

Maggie managed a tiny smile. "Sure."

They walked in silence to the outdoor dining area, where a couple of undergrads set spaghetti and meatballs on the table, along with a large salad.

Maggie flopped down at the table, and Terri sat across from her.

Bruce's vacant seat screamed his absence.

Maggie swallowed. "It's hard to believe."

"Yeah."

"And just… hard when a friend lets you down."

"Yeah." Terri looked down at the plate in front of her. "Still, at least we know he wasn't behind the attacks." She shook her head. "He was just behaving so strangely. I guess we all make mistakes, but…what a doozy."

"At least he stepped forward and told the police what he knew. That's what you said, right?"

Terri nodded. "Yeah."

A ruckus came from a nearby trailer. Maggie jumped to her feet and led Terri to the little group of people gathering near the commotion.

"What do you mean?" Luke Adakai stood in front of Bruce's trailer. His eyes were wild as they locked onto Jason.

Maggie whirled to Terri. "That's Luke! What in the world is he doing here?"

Jason stood tall, his face stony. "I mean, Bruce is in police custody. The Navajo police kept him for questioning. Look, I'm sorry he didn't call you back or whatever." He scoffed. "I'd say he had good reason."

Luke took a step back. "Bruce was arrested?" The tension on Luke's face relaxed.

Jason looked to the group that had gathered. "Well, are we gonna eat, or stand around gawking?"

Some undergrads laughed, but they dispersed.

Maggie hurried up to Luke. "Hey, it sounds like you wanted to talk to Bruce. Anything I can help you with?" She touched his arm. "Would you like to join us for dinner?"

Terri clapped him on the shoulder. "C'mon, it's spaghetti. Who doesn't love spaghetti?"

Between the two of them, they shepherded Luke to the table, where he took a seat beside Terri. Their plates piled high with pasta, salad, and garlic toast, Maggie focused on Luke.

"This is good. Who does your cooking?"

Maggie sipped her iced tea. "We take turns."

Terri's eyebrows shot up. "All except Jason. He's forbidden from going anywhere near the stove."

Maggie laughed. "Right. He's on permanent dishwashing duty."

Luke lifted his lips into a meager smile and met Maggie's eyes. He squared his shoulders and leaned towards her. "You know, if you meant what you said about building a friendship, you could help me with something."

Maggie brightened. "Of course."

"I was going to talk to Bruce Adams about something that happened at the trading post." He shrugged one shoulder. "We found a paper sack next to the register. I guess some customer took a potsherd for a souvenir, then felt remorse. They left it in the sack and wrote 'Sorry' on the outside. I wasn't sure what to do with it."

"Oh." Maggie and Terri launched into an explanation of how to handle the stolen souvenir, what a shame it was that it was taken, and that it would have to be reprocessed and relegated to a labeled box, since they didn't know what site it was found in.

The three of them chatted through dinner.

"This was nice, Luke." Maggie's voice softened. "Let's do this again soon."

He cast his gaze down at his plate and nodded. "Yes. This was nice."

Maggie and Terri cleared the table, carrying the dishes to the kitchen trailer.

Terri leaned in to Maggie. "Well, since when is he Mr. Nice Guy? You said he froze you out both times you tried to talk to him."

Maggie shrugged. "I know. But I told him I really wanted to get to know him. Maybe he's had time to calm down and process everything. If he's trying, I want to give him a chance." She felt her face soften. "I'd love to have a brother, you know?"

Terri sighed and started for the door. "No, I don't. I have three."

Luke still sat at the table and threw a smile to them as they approached. "Thanks for all the information you gave me on handling the returned potsherd. I'll get that dealt with tomorrow." His dark eyes landed on Maggie. "But could we talk?"

Maggie startled. "Okay. Want to head to my trailer?"

Terri held up her hands. "I'm gonna leave you two to yourselves. I think I heard everyone else is getting together for a game of poker. So, I'm heading to my trailer to watch a movie." She threw a peace sign over her shoulder. "See ya'."

Maggie waved. "See you in the morning."

As they walked toward Maggie's trailer, Luke turned to her. "I really need to apologize, Maggie."

"Oh?" She opened her trailer door and led him inside.

"Yes. For my harsh words when you showed me Dad's necklace. I shouldn't have reacted that way." Luke swallowed. "I heard about the attempts on your life and your injury." He gestured to Maggie's bandaged arm. "It's terrifying. It made me realize what could have happened. If you'd been killed after I spoke to you like that..." He shook his head. "I'm just grateful that didn't happen." He looked into her eyes. "I need to say I'm sorry. Will you forgive me?"

A lump formed in Maggie's throat. "Of course, Luke. I'm so happy—you have no idea. There's no reason we shouldn't be close. Let's work on building a relationship." She put her hands on his shoulders and pulled him in for a hug. She felt his body tense, and she backed away. "No rush. Let's just let things happen naturally."

Luke nodded. He crossed his arms and scanned the room. His gaze fell onto the box of letters on the floor by Maggie's bed.

"Come look at everything." They sat on the edge of her bed, and she took things from the box, one by one. She lifted the squash blossom necklace and held it out to him. "I'd still like for you to have this, Luke."

He shook his head. "No, Dad left this for you. He wanted you to have it. He saved it for you—probably made it with you in mind. It's yours."

She gently laid it aside. "Thank you for saying that."

Further down in the box was a simpler necklace. A silver cross inlaid with mother-of-pearl. "I guess he made this after he got on the Jesus Road."

Luke's face hardened for a moment.

He touched the stack of letters. "So, these are the letters he sent to your mother over the years?"

"Yes." She took them from the box. "Most of them are dated from the time shortly after my mother went back to Albuquerque, but he continued to send a couple of letters every year, mostly letting her know he wanted visits with me." Maggie hung her head. "It's been quite a shock and disappointment to find out how my mother treated and abandoned him. I'm having a hard time dealing with it."

She laid a hand on top of the stack of letters.

"It's been like getting to know our father, at least a little. In the last letter I read, he mentioned he was getting sick—having terrible fatigue and stomach pain. He was unable to work or go out into the community."

Luke shot her a startled glance and cleared his throat. "Getting sick, huh?"

He changed the subject. "Well, something occurred to me when I was thinking about this last night. It probably wasn't all your mother's fault. Uncle Thomas is almost militant in his traditionalism. He hates white man's culture. The way they tried to force their customs on the Navajo." He cast a sideways glance at Maggie. "I wouldn't be surprised to discover Uncle Thomas helped frighten your mother away. He can be a violent man."

Maggie's eyes widened. "I never considered that. I did see a lot of rage on his face when he told the carnival story."

Luke nodded. "Yeah. You need to be careful around Uncle Thomas."

~

Maggie flipped on the TV. It cast a crazy-quilt pattern on the shadowy walls of her dark trailer. A thud outside the door made her sit bolt upright. *I wish Jimmy were here right now.* A shuffling, then a slam against her door. Maggie grabbed her Ruger from her bedside drawer and ran to the door, hurling it open.

Merv held Uncle Thomas down and straddled him, his arm twisted hard behind his back.

"Uncle Thomas... Merv! What are you doing here?"

Merv shoved the older man against the wall and drew his service pistol. "Maggie, call the station. This man was lurking outside your trailer. I caught him peeking in your window."

"I wasn't lurking or peeking, you idiot, just trying to determine if she was still awake. Then I saw the TV was on. I'm here to talk with my niece."

"Uncle Thomas." Maggie's chest filled with anxiety.

"Merv, what are you doing here? You should still be in the hospital. You were injured yesterday."

"It was only a flesh wound. I wasn't about to leave you unguarded all night when someone's out to kill you. And I can see I made the right decision." He flashed a stern glance at her. "Maggie, call the station."

"But... this is my uncle."

"Maggie. *Call* the station."

With a hesitant sigh, she grabbed her phone from the nightstand, dialed 911, and gave information to the operator.

Headlights flashed through the open doorway. She turned to Merv. "That can't be NNPD already."

The car parked, and a figure walked toward her trailer. "Luke? You just left. What are you doing back here?"

He stepped into the halo of light filtering through her front door. "I crossed paths with Uncle Thomas'

SUV as I was leaving and—" He cut off his words and looked down at Thomas, who sat on the front steps, handcuffed. "What's going on?"

Maggie shook her head and scrunched her eyes. "It's a long story. Uncle Thomas was outside my trailer, looking in the window. He said it was because he wasn't sure if I was still up watching TV. Officer Yoyatewa had arrived a little while earlier to watch my trailer because of the attempts on my life. He uh…"

Merv's voice was flat. "I'm waiting for a superior officer to arrive on scene and assess the situation."

Thomas glared at Merv. "Barney Fife here thinks I'm a Peeping Tom—peeping at my niece."

"I've got orders to stop anybody who's even slightly suspicious. He only met Miss Beaumont yesterday." He gave Luke a slow rotation of his head. "I'm still not too sure about you, either."

Luke shook his head. "Huh… interesting."

~

Nathan pulled up to the Canyon de Chelly dig site, jumping out of the Navajo Nation Police Department SUV almost before the engine clicked off. Long, purposeful strides carried him to the steps of Maggie's trailer.

Yoyetewa, Maggie, and Luke stood above Thomas Adakai, who sat cuffed on the stairs.

"Yoyetewa, give me a report."

After being briefed on the situation, Nathan let out a sigh and said, "Alright, Yoyetewa, you can uncuff him for the time being."

Thomas rubbed his wrists. "This is beyond belief. I just came by here to visit my niece. I felt we had some unfinished business and…"

Nathan gave him a sharp look. "What kind of business?"

"You were there, Yazzie. You know how things took a bad turn during my conversation with Maggie. I just wanted to smooth things over."

Luke stepped closer to Maggie. Nathan heard him whisper, "Remember what I told you. You need to be careful with Uncle Thomas."

Nathan stopped in his tracks, staring down at Luke's leg, at the thin white gauze peeking from the edge of his jeans. "What's that, Mr. Adakai?"

Luke flinched. "What? What are you talking about?"

"Your leg. Is that a bandage I see below your pant leg?"

Luke's eyes widened. He shrugged his shoulders and sputtered. "This? Oh, nothing. I had a little accident on my dirt bike. It's nothing really."

Nathan pulled Luke's pant leg up a few inches, examining the bandage.

Luke's eyes blazed. "What do you think you're doing" He shoved Nathan's hand away.

"Actually, I'd like to have that looked at by a doctor. Who bandaged it for you?"

Luke glared at Nathan. "I bandaged it myself. I told you, I cut it up riding my dirt bike yesterday."

Thomas whirled around, interrupting Nathan. "So, are we under arrest or not, *Officer*?" He spat the word with contempt.

Nathan turned to him, steeling his features. Without looking at Maggie, he asked, "Ms. Beaumont, would you like to file charges?"

Maggie wrapped her arms around her middle as her uncle's gaze fell on her, dark with anger and what looked like hurt and disappointment.

"No." She shook her head. "I don't want to press charges."

Without a word, Thomas spun on his heel and stormed away from the trailer.

Luke tilted his head, a half-smile curving his lips. "Yeah, Uncle Thomas has quite a temper." He squeezed her shoulder and stepped down the stairs. "I'll see you, Sis."

Nathan hovered near Maggie, watching until the two men's cars were out of sight. Finally, his shoulders relaxed. "Are you okay?"

She gave a sharp nod. "Yes. I mean, Uncle Thomas was just—"

Nathan lifted her chin, forcing her to look at him. "Just nothing. Look, Maggie. I hate to have to say this. I understand you wanting to connect with this side of your family, but you don't know these men."

Maggie jerked her head away from his hand. "And I can't get to know them like this." She swept a hand to encompass both men in front of her. "I'd only started making progress. My brother and uncle come to see me, and you ran them off." Her voice broke on the last word, and she fisted her hands.

"Maggie... you don't know them and they're behaving suspiciously. This is the same as the artifacts at your father's—"

"Don't." Her sharp voice cut him off. "Do not say a *word* about my dad." She leaned up into his face, hers red and eyes wet. "He did not sell artifacts. He—"

"Is a man you don't know, didn't know. You're just assuming the best of him, like you are with Luke and Thomas." He closed his eyes and sighed. "It's an admirable trait, most of the time. Just don't let it get you hurt."

Nathan set his hands on his hips. "I understand your feelings, but I did what I had to do. Someone's trying to kill you. I can't take chances with anyone."

At his side, Yoyetewa piped in. "There's already been too many close calls."

She shoved back her hair. The fight went out of her posture.

Nathan ran a hand down his face. "You're still coming to my mom's tomorrow?"

She hesitated. "Yes. I'll be there."

Nathan clapped Merv's back. "Good job, Merv. I'll see you at the station in the morning."

He turned back to Maggie. "And you, keep your door locked."

~

Nathan glanced up from his coffee and waved Merv to take a seat opposite him. Nathan pushed the untouched paper cup at his elbow in front of the rookie.

Merv took a long pull of the coffee.

"The rest of the night was quiet?"

The rookie nodded. "Yeah. I watched all night and no one else showed up. The TV stayed on a while, then the trailer was quiet and dark 'til morning. Maggie went to breakfast right before I left."

"Good. What are your thoughts on the incident last night?"

Merv sat up straighter, eyes wide as a deer's in the headlights. "Oh. Um." He paused. "Well, the uncle claimed he came to see his niece and smooth things over. It's possible, but it'd be a coincidence with everything else lately."

Nathan nodded.

"And I figured it was better to be safe than sorry. I guess we didn't have enough to arrest him, but Maggie needed protecting. She's really vulnerable to these people. She wants so badly to connect with her father's family, and I don't trust either of them." He paused.

"Luke just showing up again like that? It felt off. Too convenient. I guess he visited her earlier and ate dinner with her. He said he passed the uncle's car on his way out and came back to check on her, but..." He shook his head. "The whole thing was just weird, Sergeant."

Nathan scratched his jaw. "Good insights. And honestly, I feel the same way. I'm suspicious of them both at this point."

Yoyetewa relaxed back into his chair and took another swallow of coffee. He nodded.

"Yoyetewa, you've done well. Most rookies don't get thrown into the deep end like this. I didn't spend more than an hour away from my training officer the first month I was on the job." He tilted his head. "So, I'll ask you a question. What do you think about Luke Adakai's injury?"

Merv looked down at his cup. "Well, it could be true. But I'm doubtful." He frowned. "When the assailant ran you off the road, you guys fired a few shots. The techs think the attacker was bleeding when he ran for the SUV. Maybe Luke was the one in that vehicle, and he got an injury to his leg when Maggie fired at him."

Nathan nodded. "I was thinking the same thing."

They both sipped their coffee. Merv tried to cover a yawn.

Nathan leaned forward. "Yoyetewa—"

A call came from the doorway.

"Sergeant Yazzie. Officer Yoyetewa."

Nathan turned to see Detective Deschene standing behind him, a folder in hand. "We got an update about the incident with the cruiser off Highway 7." He tossed the folder onto the desk and Nathan opened it.

"That's the results from analyzing the tire tracks on scene. There wasn't much to work with and the rain complicated matters, but they managed a decent print. They also found paint from the assailant's vehicle that transferred onto the cruiser. They could find a likely match."

Nathan's head snapped up to Deschene, silently begging the unflappable man to hurry to the point. "And the owner?"

"They think the shooter may have been driving an SUV belonging to Thomas Adakai."

Nathan let out a slow breath. *We shouldn't have let him go last night.*

He pushed to his feet. "We'll find him and the SUV."

"Sure thing, Sarge—" Another yawn interrupted Merv's words.

Deschene shook his head. "No way."

"But—"

"He's right," Nathan said. "You won't do anyone any good until you get some sleep. I'll take care of this."

Merv frowned, but he grabbed his jacket and headed for the door. "I'll check in with you later, Sergeant."

Nathan turned back to Deschene. "Do we have an address for Thomas Adakai?"

"No. Just his Flagstaff address."

"I'll call Maggie Beaumont. He may have told her."

"Good idea." Deschene threw a wave over his shoulder. "If he's the assailant, he shot two of our officers. Go get him twice as hard."

Deschene's words in a flat voice sent a shiver down Nathan's spine. He grabbed the file and pushed away from the table.

"By the way, have you heard any news about Sarah Nez?"

"She's out of ICU. It looks like she's gonna be okay."

Nathan smiled and nodded. "That's great news."

He dialed Maggie's number, but the call didn't connect. He growled as he saw that his phone had no bars.

Well, looks like I'm picking you up early, Maggie.

~

Nathan drove his pickup onto the gravel road at Canyon de Chelly, heading towards Maggie's trailer. A plume of dust trailed behind him all the way up the driveway. He'd never understand how it could rain torrentially and then be dusty a couple of days later.

He hoped Maggie could tell him where her uncle, Thomas Adakai, was staying. Nathan had a lot of questions for the man, and most importantly, he wanted to look at his SUV.

This would have been good training for Merv. If the rookie hadn't been up all night guarding Maggie, he'd have brought him along.

Nathan arrived at Maggie's trailer and stepped out of the truck. He surveyed the area. There was no way to know exactly where she was working today. He decided to try calling her again, and to his surprise, her phone rang.

"Ya'at'eeh, Officer Yazzie."

Just the sound of her voice brought a smile to his face. "Ya'at'eeh, Maggie Beaumont. I tried to call you this morning, but the call dropped."

"Well, you're coming in loud and clear right now."

"Yeah. I guess that could be because I'm sitting right here on the steps of your trailer." He was still smiling. "Could you spare a few minutes of your time to talk with me? I'm trying to track down your Uncle Thomas."

The line went silent.

"Maggie?"

"Yes. Sit tight. I'll be right there."

Nathan pocketed his phone and bent down, his elbows resting on his knees. He looked up to see

Maggie strolling toward him, her shiny, dark ponytail swinging with her stride.

He stood up. "I hope I didn't interrupt you in the middle of something important. I'll try not to keep you long."

She stopped in front of him at the bottom of the steps. "No. In fact, I was about to call it a day. My skinned-up arm's really hurting. I think I've had all I can take for today." She walked up the stairs. "Let's go inside where it's cooler."

Maggie led him through the door. "Sit down, Nathan. Would you like a cold water, or iced tea? I have both."

"Water's fine."

She opened a bottle and handed it to him. "You said you want to talk to me about Uncle Thomas?" She sat next to him on the small sofa. "I doubt there's anything I can help you with." She paused. "He only came to smooth things over with me."

"I was hoping he'd mentioned to you where he's staying. There's a few important questions I need to ask him."

Her eyes lit up. "As a matter of fact, he did mention he's staying with Luke. That's the good news. The bad news is, I have no idea where Luke lives."

"Well, that will be easy enough to find out." After getting the address for Luke Adakai from dispatch, Nathan tucked his notebook away. "Okay, I'm off to pay Thomas a visit. Too bad you aren't ready to go. You could ride along with me and then on to my mom's place."

Maggie jumped up. "If you give me ten minutes to shower and change clothes, I'll be ready. Everything else is good to go."

"Okay." Nathan looked at his watch. "Ten minutes."

She grabbed a change of clothes from her bag and ran into the bathroom.

~

Nathan pulled up in front of Luke's run-down duplex and saw Thomas's black Durango SUV in the driveway.

"Looks like Thomas is here." He pushed his sunglasses to the top of his head. "Do you want to come in? I imagine this will get ugly, knowing Thomas and his attitude."

"Yes, I'm coming in. If nothing else, I'd like for Uncle Thomas to know that I sincerely wanted to have a relationship with him—that I wasn't out to entrap him."

"Okay. Well, just go in knowing that I'm gonna ask him some questions he won't like. It won't be a pleasant visit."

She nodded, and Nathan turned off the engine.

They walked into the front yard—nothing but red dirt and gravel, with a few weeds spiking up here and there. Nathan made straight for Thomas's SUV and examined the grille. It was dented, and the cover on the right headlight broken. White paint transfer from the NNPD cruiser extended across the fender. Nathan took out his phone and made a full circle of the vehicle, snapping pictures.

He ran his fingers over the white paint and looked at Maggie, his face grim. *White paint. Exactly where it would've hit us. This isn't circumstantial—it's direct.*

He blew out a resigned sigh. Saying nothing, he strode to the front door, Maggie a step behind.

Nathan squared his shoulders and rapped on the door. A few moments later, it opened and Dan Hoskie stood before him, one arm in a jacket. "Officer Yazzie. Maggie. If you're here to see Luke, he's at work right now. I was just about to leave, but…"

Maggie took a step closer. "I'd forgotten Luke had a roommate."

Nathan looked past Dan. "We're actually here to speak with Thomas."

Dan nodded. "Sure thing." He tugged his jacket straight and waved him inside.

"I have to leave. Goodnight."

Through the open door, they saw Thomas standing in the living room. His face registered surprise, then his usual angry frown.

"Ya'at'eeh, Thomas. Can we come in for a few minutes?"

Thomas's posture stiffened. "Well, I was about to get on the road too, but yeah, I guess you can come in."

Nathan noted a suitcase sitting near the hallway. "You heading back to Flagstaff?"

"Yeah. I came here to meet my brother's daughter, and I've done that." He peered at Maggie from under his lowered brow. "I came by to say goodbye last night, but that didn't go well, thanks to your bumbling young partner."

Maggie opened her mouth to speak, then looked at Nathan. They weren't here to have this conversation right now. "Uncle Thomas, I just want you to believe one thing. I sincerely wanted to build a close relationship with both you and Luke. I'm sorry it didn't turn out that way."

Nathan cleared his throat. "Thomas, I do have some official business I need to talk to you about. Can we sit down for a few minutes?"

Thomas drew his brows together in a deep frown. "Sure, I guess so. Have a seat."

Nathan and Maggie sat on an old brown floral pattern couch that must have been purchased at a yard sale. Thomas sat stiffly on the edge of a non-matching red plaid chair.

"Okay. What are we talking about?"

Nathan drew in a deep breath. No point in putting it off. He dove right in. "When we pulled up just now, I noticed your Durango's been in an accident. It has fresh white paint transfer, and a broken headlight. How did that happen?"

Thomas straightened. "Huh? I don't know anything about accident damage. Let me go look—you gotta be making this up."

If Thomas was lying, he was doing a great job of it. Nathan watched his every expression, the dilation of his pupils, the tone of his voice.

"Two nights ago, someone ambushed Maggie and me in the desert. A black SUV rammed our cruiser from behind and ran us off the road. Your vehicle has evidence of being the one that struck us."

Thomas's face went slack. "I haven't been anywhere since I got to Chinle except your mom's place and to Maggie's trailer last night. I didn't run anybody off the road—especially not a police cruiser." Thomas leaned forward, voice rising in volume.

"Mr. Adakai—"

"This is, is ridiculous. Ask Luke, his neighbors, anyone. I was home the night before last." He shook his head, then turned to Maggie. "Surely you can't believe this."

Maggie's eyes went wide. She clenched her hands around her purse. "Well, I—"

"What?" Thomas' face contorted. "You too? You'd expect the worst, that level of betrayal, from your own family?" He turned away. "The betrayal here is yours."

He straightened his shoulders and looked only at Nathan. "Are you arresting me, Officer?"

Nathan shook his head. "No, but we'll be investigating you. You need to stay in Chinle for the duration of the investigation, but I'm not arresting you."

Thomas gripped the back of the chair, knuckles white as he leaned over it, body tense. "Then get out."

Chapter Nine

Maggie wrapped her arms around herself and leaned against the wall of the duplex. Maybe she could physically hold herself together.

They walked to the Tahoe, and she climbed into the passenger seat.

Beside her, Nathan paused before starting the engine. "Maggie?"

She bit her lip.

"Hey, are you okay?"

She dragged in a breath. "I've been better."

He patted her hand. "I told you this would be rough. We've both witnessed Thomas's anger even before today. And it was to be expected. I mean, I just insinuated that he tried to kill his brother's daughter. Yeah... the man's gonna be angry."

Nathan started the engine and pulled out into traffic. They rode silently for several minutes.

"You're awfully quiet. You seem more upset by that interview than I am." Maggie turned slightly in her seat as she spoke to him.

"I've been puzzling this out. Thomas could have been lying. What do you think, Maggie? You were there, even though it was dark, and you were terrified. Do you believe it was Thomas who attacked us in the desert?"

She pushed her hair behind her ear. "You know, now that I really think about it, I believe the man that chased us was pretty slender. And fast. He ran like a gazelle. Somehow, I can't see Uncle Thomas being the one that ran after us that night."

~

Maggie stowed her belongings in the corner of the spare bedroom before flopping into a chair. She folded her hands in her lap and stared into the semi-darkness of the room.

She loved Nathan's family, but she didn't feel totally at home here. Maggie sorely wished she was back in her own trailer with a cup of tea and reading the last of her dad's letters. She missed Terri, even Bruce, and their cozy, shared dinners.

Maggie eyed her belongings and her father's cardboard box. She picked up the VHS tape and looked at it. She had no idea what was on it. *Maybe that's why I still haven't watched it.* It could be something special that helped her know her dad better, or it could be an old movie he'd taped for himself. *God, please let it be something with my father's voice on it. I want to see his face and hear him speak so very much.*

The sudden realization came to her, that she'd been doing this a lot lately—whispering little prayers. She'd never done it before, but something felt so different inside her now. Something she didn't understand and couldn't put into words.

A tap at the bedroom door startled her from her reverie, and she hurried to open it. Nathan, Wanda, and Jimmy stood on the other side, all smiling, including the brown mutt. He ran into the room and hopped up on her legs, begging for attention.

Maggie laughed out loud. "Jimmy, I've missed you the past couple of days." She stooped down and scratched him enthusiastically.

Nathan and Wanda stepped inside the room, and Wanda set a fragrant cup of tea on the bedside table.

"Mom brought you a little something to make you feel more at home."

"You love tea," Wanda said in her stilted English.

He pointed at Jimmy. "And I wanted to bring you something, too."

Maggie stood up and gave them a broad smile. "Thank you both so much. Honestly, I was feeling a little lonely and displaced."

Jimmy flopped down on the floor. "Mom says he can stay with you tonight if you want him to." Nathan lowered his voice conspiratorially. "I convinced her you need him as part of your guard team."

Maggie looked at Wanda. "Thank you so much, Mrs. Yazzie." She nodded. "Yes, I'd love to keep Jimmy with me."

Wanda left the room and Nathan sat in the wooden, straight-back chair. "Mom could see you were pretty down in the dumps. She wanted to make you feel welcome."

"Oh, Nathan. Please tell her how much I appreciate her gestures. It means so much to me."

He gave her a slow grin. "I think you got that message across to Mom with that beautiful smile of yours."

She felt heat rise in her cheeks. "Well. Anyway. I'm going to drink my tea and read the last three of my dad's letters tonight. I'll be sad to come to the end of his little messages to me and my mother. And after I finish reading these, I have one VHS tape in the box that I haven't looked at yet. I just hope and pray that he speaks on the tape. I'd love to hear his voice."

Nathan nodded. "I can only imagine what you must be feeling right now. I hope your dad's on that tape, too." He stood up and walked to the door. "Well, Mom and I are going to go sit outside and watch the stars for a while. If you decide to come out with us later, you're more than welcome."

"Thank you."

With a smile, Nathan closed the door behind him. Maggie pulled out her favorite throw and the last letters. She sat down in the chair with the blanket over her lap and Jimmy at her feet.

Each word in her father's handwriting tugged at Maggie's heart, but the last message stopped her cold.

April 28, 2024

Dear Jackie,

All the letters I've sent to you have come back to me, at first with you writing "return to sender" and later marked with "not at this address." I have no other address for you, so I suppose I'll just have to hope that, by some miracle, this one finds its way through. I don't know what else to do.

While I'm only forty-nine years old, I fear I don't have much time. I've never seen my daughter, never glimpsed her smile, nor talked to her. Margaret never heard me tell her I loved her, that I always have, since before she was born. I'm asking that you give me one chance for that now. I want to see her, tell her, give her the necklace I made her. I just want to meet her, Jackie. Just one time for her to come and see me.

As I mentioned before, I've been sick. Things only seem to be getting worse. I feel so exhausted and have terrible stomach pains. I can't keep any food down. I've lost so much weight you wouldn't recognize me, Jackie. I never have enough breath, I am confused all the time, and as weak as a kitten.

I just want to see Margaret. To be with family at the end. I can't reach Thomas, but my son checks in on me each week. One of the workers at the trading post said fermented foods helps with nausea. I have been eating olives every day to help, but it hasn't been enough.

I've had no alcohol. Not in decades, but sometimes I wonder if this is a consequence of that. I've done nothing else. But it gets worse. If I didn't know better, I'd think someone was poisoning me.

Anyway. It feels like time is short, Jackie. If you won't come see me, please at least send Margaret. Please.

Love always,
John

~

Poisoned. The word pulsed in Maggie's mind. She read the sentence again. *If I didn't know better, I'd think someone was poisoning me.* It hit her like a bolt of lightning. Could that be the explanation? Was John Adakai a victim of poisoning?

She crumpled the letter in her hand and headed out of the bedroom, through the kitchen and bounded to the back door, Jimmy at her heels.

Maggie threw open the door, slamming it against the side of the house. Nathan and Wanda spun towards her, eyes filled with alarm.

"Nathan! Look at this." She shoved the letter at him.

"Maggie, take it easy. Let's go inside. I can't read this out here in the dark."

The three of them gathered around the dimly lit kitchen table, and Nathan read the letter aloud. As he read the part where John described his symptoms, a line formed between Nathan's brows. He read the most troubling sentence. *"If I didn't know better, I'd think someone was poisoning me."*

Nathan spoke again to Wanda, explaining everything in Dine'.

She listened, shook her head violently, and shouted, "No."

Nathan turned slowly to Maggie. "My mother says she's *always* believed John was murdered."

Maggie's world tilted. She stood up and paced the kitchen floor. "What's this all about, Nathan? Why would anyone want to kill my father?" She stopped in her tracks and clutched the back of the dining chair.

Nathan shook his head. "I don't know yet, Maggie, but it could be because of the artifacts found on his property. They'd be worth a king's ransom on the black market."

She whirled around to him. "Nathan, can I borrow your truck? I know it's a big request, but I want to go to the mobile home and get that jar of olives that's still sitting in the back of the refrigerator. Can we have those tested for poison?"

"I'll go get them. I doubt anyone will be there tonight. They couldn't do any more digging until daylight."

"I need to come with you to see things for myself. I'll be able to tell if anything's been tampered with."

Nathan hesitated, then took her by the arm. "Alright. But you stay by my side the whole time, understand? No wandering off, no taking risks. If anything seems off, we're getting out of there. Got it?"

Maggie nodded. "Yes, thank you. I promise I'll stay close."

Nathan spoke to his mother briefly, then turned back to Maggie. "Come on. We can take the SUV. Let's get this done."

They drove down the long, hard-packed dirt road toward the highway, the headlights of the NNPD Tahoe slicing through the blackness of night.

Maggie spoke into the silence. "Why would they go after him? The only change he mentioned was the olives, but..."

Nathan's hands tightened on the steering wheel. "Yeah."

"So, who could have poisoned him" Her voice was weak.

"You know, Maggie."

She closed her eyes. "Uncle Thomas and..."

"And?"

"And Luke." She shook her head. "But they wouldn't."

He met her eyes. "Who else?"

"I don't know. Maybe. Maybe whoever sold the olives or—"

"That doesn't make sense." He lowered his voice. "I'm sorry, but the people who surrounded him, the ones who've been acting suspiciously, are Thomas and Luke. It must hurt to meet new family and discover this kind of dysfunction, but so far, all the evidence points to one, or both, of them. They're the ones we've been looking at."

She met his eyes again. "Been looking at? All along?" She raised her voice. "Why didn't you say anything?"

He blew out a tired sigh. "I figured I didn't need to. You've seen it. Think about what happened outside your place at the canyon. Sneaking around your trailer at night, the damage on Thomas's vehicle. And Luke? You shot at your attacker and injured him, then the next day Luke shows up with a bandage around his leg?"

Maggie paused and swallowed the lump in her throat. Her hands trembled, and she sat on them to stop their shaking. "Sure. I guess so."

Nathan patted her knee. "You'll get through this. We'll find out what happened."

"Thank you." She squeezed his hand. "I feel better knowing you're here with me."

"Anytime."

As they approached the lane to her father's mobile home, Maggie's body tensed. A silver coupe sat at the end of her access road, its headlights glaring into the night.

~

Nathan lost precious seconds staring at the car as it turned onto the highway and sped back the way he had come.

Maggie clenched the armrest. "What was—"

"I'm not sure. There's no reason for anyone to be on that road." He used Maggie's driveway to pull a quick U-turn, gravel spitting against the bottom of the SUV.

Speeding up, he reached the back of the car in his headlights. He flipped on the light bar, throwing a haze of red and blue over the highway. Within moments, the vehicle signaled and pulled onto the shoulder.

Nathan parked behind the car at an angle and eased the door open. "Stay in the car."

With caution, he came around the side of the coupe and approached the driver's window. "The property down the road is part of an active investigation. What were you—"

Inside the car, FBI special agent Elise Martin sat in a crisp white blouse and pencil skirt. Her blazer lay on the passenger seat, a manila envelope perched on top. "Officer Yazzie."

Nathan schooled his features and relaxed his body language. "Agent Martin, what were you doing at the Adakai property this evening?"

She raised one thin eyebrow. "I could ask you the same." She glanced at the folder. "I'm bringing some requested files to Lieutenant Benally. I turned down the wrong access road." She raised one shoulder in a delicate half-shrug.

"Okay." He cleared his throat. "I was taking Ms. Beaumont to the property to pick up something she left behind." He gestured back to Maggie, who leaned out the window of the NNPD vehicle to watch the conversation.

Agent Martin nodded. "Well, if you have no further questions...?"

He waved a hand. "Of course. Have a good evening."

He trudged back to the SUV and climbed in as the silver BMW sped off. Just managing to keep his head off the steering wheel until the taillights faded, his forehead met the leather with a *thunk*.

Uncle Ben never, ever, would have made a mistake like that.

"Nathan?"

He scrunched his eyes shut, then sat up. He shifted into drive and started back towards the mobile home.

"Nathan, are you okay?"

"Yeah. Fine." *Sort of.*

"What was that back there?" Maggie asked gently.

"Just me screwing up in front of an FBI agent and letting everyone down. Classic Nathan."

"I've never seen you screw up."

He stared at the road. "Let's drop it."

"I saw you trusting your instincts. You've saved lives, found clues—you didn't let anyone down."

He shook his head. "You don't understand. My uncle, Benjamin Benally—he's a legend. And I'm...not."

She rested a hand on his arm, grounding him.

"You're not your uncle. And you're just starting out."

He exhaled, rolling down the window for the night air. "I've felt the pressure to live up to him my whole life."

"Well." He glanced her way and caught her grin in the dim glow of the dashboard lights. "Go easy on yourself. I think you're pretty awesome."

He glanced at her, smile tugging at his lips. "Thanks. You're not too bad yourself."

They eased to a stop in front of the mobile home, stooped under the yellow police tape, and unlocked the door. Instead of the dusty, stale smell that usually assaulted Nathan's nose when he entered the mobile home, he noticed the lingering scents of coffee and a whisper of Maggie's cologne.

He stepped inside first, Maggie close behind.

Nathan pulled a flashlight from his duty belt. "Don't turn on the lights." He scanned the room. "Let me look around before you do anything."

"Okay."

He slid his service pistol from its holster and secured the mobile home. "Alright, go ahead. Get the jar of olives."

Maggie opened the refrigerator and pulled out a half-gallon size jar of green cocktail olives, almost empty.

Nathan's jaw dropped. "Wow! He wasn't kidding about eating olives, was he?"

"No. If these things are poison, he ate most of them, thinking he was helping himself get better."

He could hear the pain in her voice and softened his tone. "Is there anything else you need to get while we're here?"

"Nothing I can think of."

Nathan turned to her. "I'm going to take a quick look in that shed to see if anything's been disturbed." He started for the back door. "Don't you move."

She stood straight and saluted him. "Yes, sir."

"I mean it."

"I know, I'll wait here."

He sighed and walked out the door.

As Nathan approached the old wooden storage building, he noted the peeling green paint and door standing ajar. Surely the NNPD hadn't left the door open?

He gave it a gentle nudge, then flashed his light around the room. Empty.

No people, no boxes, nothing different from the last time he'd entered the shed...except the footprints.

The faint outline of muddy shoes tracked from the door to the shelves at the back. Nathan leaned down and examined them with his flashlight. He snapped a few pictures to document the new find. Bruce Adam's face flashed in his memory. Did these prints belong to the middle-man who picked up the artifacts Bruce excavated? If so, he'd surely been disappointed this time.

~

"More rain? You've gotta be kidding me. With these storms, the canyons will never dry up." Thunderheads gathered above them as Nathan and Maggie strolled from the Police Tahoe into the Chinle Police Department, John Adakai's jar of olives in a paper sack.

Maggie winked at him. "Another male storm coming in."

Nathan led the way to his uncle's office and touched the nameplate on the door—Lt. Benjamin Benally. *It should read The Great Benjamin Benally.*

A tap on the door, then Nathan turned the knob. "Lieutenant, could we get Deschene and Yoyetewa in here? I have some fresh evidence we need to discuss and get processed."

"Call 'em in here and take a seat." Ben rolled back from his desk and refilled his mug. He held it up and glanced from Maggie to Nathan. "Want one?"

"No thank you, Lieutenant." Maggie touched her stomach. "I'm floating in coffee right now."

Nathan shook his head.

Detective Deschene and Merv strode in and stood over Nathan.

"What is it? You said you have new evidence?" Merv pulled a chair up next to Maggie.

Nathan set the bag containing the olives on Ben's desk and pulled John Adakai's letter from his pocket. "Listen to this."

He read John's letter aloud to the group, then removed the olive jar from its sack. "I think we need to enter these into evidence and have them analyzed right away."

Deschene blew out a slow, noisy breath. "Hmm. So, John bought these and ate them every day for his health. Luke visited every week. It seems like he was the only other person in the house." He looked at Maggie. "Do you think Luke is capable of something like this? That would mean he murdered his own father."

Maggie shook her head. "I honestly don't know. I just met Luke a few days ago. He's intense, and an incredibly angry person. I hate to think it's possible. I hope not. I mean... his own father! It appeared Luke loved him very much."

Merv leaned forward in his chair. "But Maggie, most victims know the person who murders them. It's entirely possible that Luke poisoned his father. No, we couldn't rule him out." Nathan shot him a sidelong 'shut up' glance, and Merv sat back in his chair.

Maggie rubbed her palms over her jeans. "One thing I should mention, though. When Luke came to visit me, he told me more than once that our father's brother, Thomas, is almost fanatical in his dislike of White culture infiltrating the old Navajo ways. Luke seemed to feel that Uncle Thomas hated it that our dad became a practicing Christian."

Ben rubbed his cheek. "I can vouch for that. Thomas is very traditional and resented the introduction of White ways." He picked up the letter and glanced at it. "Detective, get these things into evidence and pay a visit to both Luke and Thomas."

Nathan looked up at Deschene. "I can give you Luke's address in Chinle. Thomas has been staying with him. We were out there earlier today. We talked to Thomas and his oddball roommate, who works at the trading post. Some guy by the name of Dan Hoskie."

Deschene nodded. "We'll get on it."

Nathan stood. "I'll drive out to Luke's place again first thing in the morning. I told Thomas not to leave town, and I want to make sure he's still around. Maybe I'll pay a little visit to Dan Hoskie, too."

Chapter Ten

Maggie peered through sleep-blurred eyes. A crowing rooster broke into her still-foggy brain. She rolled onto her back and stretched. The faint dawn light filtered around the edges of the sheer curtain hanging over Mrs. Yazzie's window. *So quiet and peaceful here.*

Taking her time, she got up, dressed, and shoved her feet into her old slippers—after shaking them to be certain no unwelcome visitors had made themselves at home during the night. That was the first thing she'd learned about living in the high desert. Quiet as a mouse, she opened the door, poured a cup of the coffee she'd smelled, and made her way onto the back porch.

A cool breeze caressed her as she stood looking out at the ever-present mountains. Such a beautiful morning.

Wanda and Shirley's voices drifted to her from near the brush arbor, already busy with their day. The rhythm of life here was totally organic and not dictated by an alarm clock.

Maggie settled onto the porch steps, the mug warming her fingers as Jimmy pressed close, his head nudging her lap like he belonged there. She stroked behind his ears. "Jimmy, where have you been all my life, you sweet old boy?"

With Nathan gone to the station, an odd emptiness tore at Maggie's heart. When he was near, he poured a certain energy, strength, and something else into her very being.

No. There's no point in even thinking along those lines.

She sipped her coffee, and thoughts of Bruce filled her mind. *Poor Bruce. I know he wasn't the one who injured Terri or tried to kill me. God, please help Bruce as he faces the trying process ahead of him.*

Maggie went back inside the house, grabbed her cell phone, and dialed Terri. *Please let this call connect.* Three rings, and a familiar, cheerful voice came through.

"Morning, Maggie. How's life on the sheep ranch?"

"*Ya'at'eeh abini!* That's good morning in Navajo. Does that answer your question?"

Terri snickered. "You're a goner, aren't you? Totally caught up in this new Navajo side of your identity."

"You may be right. At least, I know I love it here much more than in the city. But I called to ask you how things are going there at the dig site?"

The phone went silent. "Terri?"

"Oh, Mags. It's crazy around here. It'll be a miracle if we ever get another grant from the University. This new director is clueless."

Maggie felt herself deflate. "Okay. I know Nathan left his keys on the kitchen table. I'll come help."

"No, Maggie. You aren't safe here."

"I'll call Merv and let him know where I am."

"Maggie…"

Maggie hung up and flew into the bedroom to pull a brush through her hair, then feed Jimmy.

She scribbled a note to Shirley, or whomever else might find it, and explained she was borrowing Nathan's truck and going to the canyon for a few hours of work. Then she called Merv's cell, which thankfully went straight to voicemail, and left a message for the rookie. She sighed again. *Yeah, I'll catch it from him, too.*

With determined strides, she crossed the yard to Nathan's pickup, parked under a tree. She pushed the fob button to open the door and shushed the loud *thunk*.

The ground, still wet from the previous night's storm, showed Nathan's footprints around the truck, and now hers.

She stepped into the vehicle, adjusted the seat and mirrors, and started the engine. "Don't be angry with me, Nathan. They need help at the dig site."

Halfway down the access road, Maggie braked to a stop. A black SUV sat in the middle of the lane, blocking her path out. "What the… Who in the world is that?"

Someone squatted next to the front driver's side tire, removing the hubcap. Maggie rolled down the window and shouted to the man. "Is there anything I can do? Do you need me to call someone for you?"

The man didn't turn to her, but he spoke in a strange, raspy voice. "No, but could you give me a hand here for a minute?"

She opened the door and strode forward, unhappy with herself for the annoyance she felt. They needed her at the canyon ASAP and this vehicle stood in her way. *Terri sounded so stressed out; I should be there right now.*

As she reached the stranger, she pasted on a smile. "What can I do …"

Behind her, gravel crunched. She tried to turn, but it was too late. An arm tightened around her throat, squeezing the breath from her lungs. Maggie stumbled as she was dragged into the backseat of the pickup. She struggled with all her might, but the attacker held fast, the jostling making her dizzy.

She tried to scream, but no sound reached her mouth, not even her breath. The world around her turned dark.

~

Sheer panic coursed through Maggie's veins. She struggled as her attacker pulled a cloth bag over her head and secured her arms with duct tape. The stranger pushed her onto the floorboard of Nathan's truck, then got behind the wheel.

She could barely breathe and her injured arm burned like fire.

"Who are you? Why are you doing this to me? I have nothing you'd want."

"Oh, don't be too sure about that, Miss Beaumont. You've got some things I'm very interested in."

That voice—it was oddly familiar, even though he'd attempted to alter it and his speech pattern. "Who are you? Let me go!"

Sweat broke out on her forehead as she struggled to free her bound hands.

Her kidnapper punched numbers into his phone. "I've got her. I'll follow you to the ruins."

~

Maggie struggled, twisting her bound hands in a vain attempt to free them. They'd been driving for what seemed like hours. Every movement caused the tape to cut into her wrists and made her breathing more difficult. Finally, she lay still, resting her head against the truck's floor mat. She had to rest. Reserve her strength for whatever fight lay ahead.

Her phone had buzzed a hundred times, and she hadn't answered. She knew Terri and Merv were both frantic by now and had alerted Nathan that something was wrong.

Hot tears streamed down her cheeks.

God, please help me. My father believed, and I believe, too. Please, let Nathan find me.

Nathan. With every fiber of her being, she knew he was looking for her. She could feel it. She loved him. No point in denying it now. Suddenly, she wished she'd shared that kiss with him back at the hogan. It might be the only one they'd ever have.

The truck slowed and negotiated a sharp right-hand turn, rolling her onto her side, then proceeded over a gravelly road that jostled her until her head ached. The vehicle came to an abrupt stop, and her captor opened his door, then slammed it shut. Her heart beat furiously and sweat broke out on her from head to toe.

She heard the door of another vehicle open and the muffled voices of two men talking reached her ears. The door beside her jerked open and rough hands dragged her from the truck. Maggie fought, trying with all her strength to pull away, but a second set of hands grabbed her injured arm and pulled her blindly along.

"Who are you? Why are you doing this?" But she got no response.

After a long, stumbling climb up a rough path, they stopped under a shaded copse of trees. The temperature dropped and she could smell the green scent of Ponderosa pines and hear the wind blowing through aspens.

She screamed out her words. "Who are you? Where are you taking me? Tell me!"

Maggie reeled, her muscles turning to jelly. She didn't know where she was, she was exhausted, and she had no reasonable plan for escape. The fight went out of her, and she collapsed. The men yanked her upright and pulled her along until they shoved her to the hard ground. One set of hands jerked the cloth bag from her head and tossed it aside.

She blinked as her eyes slowly adjusted to the light surrounding her. She raised her head and peered into the face of her brother, then to the man beside him. Dan Hoskie from the trading post.

"Luke… why?"

~

Nathan turned down the vehicle's radio and picked up his ringing cell phone.

"Sergeant, it's Yoyetewa. I don't know if you've talked to her this morning, but I got a voicemail from Maggie over an hour ago, saying she was going to the canyon to work today. I called her friend Terri, and she said Maggie never showed up. We both tried to call her several times."

Nathan's gut wrenched. "Yoyetewa, I'm going back to my mom's place first, then heading for Chinle. Keep in touch with me."

He slowed his SUV, pulled a U-turn, and floored the accelerator.

Pulling up in front of his mother's house, he immediately saw that Maggie had taken his truck. No one was around. His mother and Aunt Shirley were probably out dropping hay for the sheep.

He made his way into the house and called out. "Maggie. Are you here?"

No reply.

He raced back outside and examined the ground surrounding his truck's parking space. Only his footprints and Maggie's smaller ones were visible.

Every instinct in him screamed that something wasn't right.

Nathan jumped back into his vehicle and headed toward Luke's home in Chinle.

~

Nathan pulled into the cracked driveway outside of Luke Adakai's duplex. He cut through the graveled yard, strode onto the porch, and pounded.

Thomas opened the door, his expression wary. "Sergeant Yazzie." He stepped back and waved Nathan in.

"Mr. Adakai. I need information from you. Are your nephew and his roommate around?" Nathan turned and took in the room's scuffed walls and glanced down the hallway.

"No, they're not." Thomas paused, the line deepening between his brows. "I haven't seen them this morning." He met Nathan's intense stare, concern shadowing his eyes. "And you might as well know. My SUV is gone again."

Nathan swallowed a lump in his throat. "Mr. Adakai—"

"What's happened now?" Thomas' voice was low, urgent. "You're here because something happened. Is Maggie okay?"

Nathan took a breath, held it to steady his voice. "Thomas… Maggie called a couple hours ago to say she was heading to Canyon de Chelly. She didn't show up and no one's heard from her."

Thomas dropped into the red plaid chair and put his head in his hands, a muttered curse escaping his lips.

"We're trying to find her. Believe me, my main priority is to make sure she's safe." Nathan grabbed his notepad from his pocket. "So you haven't seen Luke or Dan this morning?"

Thomas straightened and shook his head. "No."

"And your vehicle is missing?"

"Yes."

Nathan closed his notebook over his pen. "Do you think you could reach them by phone?"

Thomas picked up his cell and punched in a number. A moment later, Luke's voice filtered through the speaker as the call went straight to voicemail. Thomas tried again, dialing Dan's number with the same results.

Nathan locked eyes with Thomas, seeing the same dread that ate at his gut.

"Mr. Adakai, do you have any other idea where Luke might be?"

Thomas leaned forward, clasped his hands together until his fingers turned white. He looked up at Nathan. "Luke is my blood. My brother's child. But so is Maggie, and I haven't done right by her since the day we met."

"Where, Thomas? This is important."

He sucked in his breath and exhaled slowly, every line in his face showing his anguish as he spoke. "When I came in last night, I heard Luke and Dan in the kitchen talking about a place near the New Mexico border. When he was a kid, John and I used to take Luke exploring up there. There's a couple of old kivas hidden from plain sight. Apparently, archeologists haven't found them, and we didn't tell anyone about them. We wanted to keep them our little secret. One of them is still mostly buried, but the other has been protected—it's completely under the rim of an overhang. We could get all the way down into it and check it out." He looked at his hands. "I could tell from their conversation that they were up to no good. I thought maybe they'd found something valuable in one of the kivas, or that they planned to hide looted artifacts in them." He covered his face. "Now, I feel it's something much worse." He looked up at Nathan. "If I was going to kidnap someone, that's where I'd take them. And I'd lay odds that's where Luke is right now." He shook his head. "I've known Luke wasn't right since he was a child. He never seemed to care about anyone but himself."

Nathan's jangling phone disturbed the quiet, jolting him out of his silent terror.

"Sergeant, it's Yoyetewa. I want to update you on some developments and what not. First off, I went to the trading post to question Dan Hoskie, and it seems he was a no-show for work today. He didn't even call in.

"And Detective Deschene sent a team to your mother's property. They found Maggie's fresh footprints on the access road. Also, two sets of tire tracks, which they're comparing against the ones from the attack on Maggie and me. Both sets of muddy tire tracks turn right onto Highway 7, for whatever help that might be.

"Also, Sarge, the lab got back to us about the olives. I figured you'd want to know right away. The olives tested positive for low doses of arsenic. It looks like John Adakai died from a slow poisoning."

The air in the room froze.

Nathan dropped onto the couch but kept his eyes fixed on Thomas as he continued his phone call.

"Thanks for the update, Yoyetewa. I'm at Luke Adakai's address now. Thomas Adakai is here, and he says he hasn't seen Luke or his roommate, Dan Hoskie, since last night. I had him try to call them, but neither answered. And Thomas' SUV is missing."

Static buzzed on the line and Nathan worried the call might drop. After a moment, Yoyetewa answered. "Okay, I'll pass that on to Detective Deschene."

"And Lieutenant Benally. Finding Luke Adakai and Dan Hoskie is my number one priority. I'm afraid they've got Maggie."

The line went silent, then he heard a sharp intake of breath. "Right."

"I'm on my way to some old ruins on the New Mexico border. It's likely I won't have any service once I get up there."

"Yes, Sergeant."

Nathan disconnected the call. Thomas sat across from him, looking shellshocked. "Is there anything you've left out, Mr. Adakai? Anything at all that might help me locate Luke?"

Thomas shook his head slowly. "No. Nothing. Please, Sergeant Yazzie... go find Maggie."

Nathan stopped at the front door on his way out. "Come on, Thomas. I'll never find this place alone. You're coming with me." He met the older man's eyes. "If you want me to find Maggie, I'll need your help."

Thomas nodded. "Of course. I'll put on my hiking boots. This ain't gonna be a walk in the park." He disappeared into the bedroom, and then returned, pulling on a jacket over his worn t-shirt. "Don't worry. I'll help you find her."

The two-hour ride to the New Mexico border felt twice as long as it really was. Anxiety churned Nathan's stomach. His mind had no room for thoughts of the craggy beauty of the Chuska mountains or the greenery at their feet. They drove in silence along steep mountain roads.

"Slow down. Take the next turn." Thomas indicated a gravel road branching off to the right. Nathan slowed and executed a sharp turn onto the narrow utility road. They followed it until it dead-ended. Thomas' SUV and Nathan's pickup sat at the far end by the tree line.

Thomas popped the lock on the passenger door. "From here, we go on foot." He didn't wait for Nathan, but took off under the thin cover of trees.

Nathan paused by the door to the Tahoe. He pulled his phone from his pocket and stared at it. *If Thomas is right, this is where they're holding Maggie.*

He held down the little arrow key and scanned through his list of contacts. Pausing over Uncle Ben, he scrolled down to Mervin Yoyetewa. He shook his head. *It doesn't matter what Uncle Ben would do. I'll do this my way.*

The phone took a long moment before it connected. He checked. One bar of signal.

Static clicked over the line.

"Yoyetewa."

"We think we've found Maggie, Luke, and Dan."

"—derstand —epeat?" Yoyetewa's voice cut off. The connection was awful.

Nathan glanced through the open door at the GPS on the dashboard. Slowly, he read out the coordinates over the phone. He repeated them twice more.

"—zzie? Coordi—Maggie?"

The call dropped. Nathan stuffed the phone into his pocket.

He paused, grabbed a second set of handcuffs, and closed the door. He'd done what he could. Time to find Maggie.

Chapter Eleven

Maggie's heart lurched as Luke pulled her by her wrists to the ancient rock-strewn site. Crimson oozed from beneath the tight duct tape. The scraped flesh of her injured arm bled now, after the rough ride in the back floorboard of the truck.

She kept her eyes on the ground until they reached the edge of an ancient kiva, dug deep into the earth—probably over a thousand years old. Maggie looked first at Luke, then at Dan Hoskie, who held her upper arm in a vice-like grip. She shook her head—slowly at first, then violently. "No! What are you doing, Luke? Where are we? I'm not going down there."

Her head was light, and the world spun around her. She took a deep breath and released it.

Luke jerked her face up to him. "Oh, but you are, sis. We're all going down there. It's not so bad. You'll get to rest now."

He strode under the overhang of the rock ledge and pulled out a long ladder he'd had waiting there, then a torch. He'd planned well for this. "I'll go first, then Maggie, then you follow last, Dan."

She thrust out her bound hands. "You'll have to cut me loose."

"You can manage. Move."

Luke lowered the ladder over the side of the broken rock wall that surrounded the opening in the ground. He switched on the flashlight on his cell phone and beamed it down into the kiva. He turned a lopsided grin at Maggie. "Just let me check for rattlers before I start down the ladder."

Maggie heaved a ragged cry and swiped away tears.

Luke took a lighter from his pocket and lit the torch. It flamed brightly in the early evening light. He stepped over the edge of the low rock wall and onto the ladder.

Dan pushed Maggie forward with a rough shove. "You next."

She grabbed the top of the ladder with her bound hands, then climbed over the edge onto the first foothold she could reach. After a few clumsy steps, Dan followed.

She fumbled down the ladder. After about ten feet, the air grew cooler.

At the bottom of the kiva, Maggie looked around the dark circular space, eyes slowly adjusting to the dim light. She inhaled the scent of earth, stone, ancient wood, and ashes. She instantly recognized the features of an ancient ceremonial kiva, somehow yet unexplored by archeologists. *God help me. Will this place be my grave?*

Luke pulled his backpack from his shoulders and dropped it to the ground. Against the wall lay a stack of wood he must've stored there. He threw several logs into a firepit in the middle of the underground room. Luke lit them, and they blazed to life.

Maggie gazed around the subterranean pit. Every inch of the walls, covered in precisely hand-fitted stone. In the center of the space, a rock firepit, now blazing. Along the perimeter, a ledge circled the wall. She knew this place would have originally had a domed roof, and that entry would have been via a ladder that descended through that portal.

Dan shoved her hard. She fell onto the ledge, catching herself with her taped hands.

The flames in the firepit licked up, casting eerie shadows on the stone walls. Faded traces of ancient murals still showed on the borders. Kachinas, bent and dancing their ritual dances. In her imagination, she could see the old ones circling the firepit, performing their ceremonies and hear their ghostly chants.

She sat up straight and screamed at Luke. "Why?"

Luke dropped onto the stone bench near Maggie. He tilted his head, a smirk on his face. "Why what, Maggie?"

She laughed—sharp, brittle, on the edge of hysteria. "Why kidnap me? Scare me half to death? Why do all of this?"

Amusement gleamed in his black eyes. "To death, indeed." He leaned back and crossed his arms. "It seems you're missing the bigger picture here." He tilted his head. "Shouldn't your question be, 'Why cut my brakes?' or 'Why force me off the road?'"

Maggie's heart turned to lead, sinking to the bottom of her stomach. "No."

"Or perhaps, 'Why run me off the land Dad willed me?' That one would cut right to the heart of the matter."

"No!" She squeezed her eyes shut and averted her gaze.

"And yet."

A sound echoed from above. Luke and Dan whirled toward the entrance portal. Sunset beamed through the entrance.

Dan turned to Luke. "You hear that? Are you sure no one followed us?"

"Yeah, I heard... something. Nobody could be on our trail this fast. No one else knows about this place but Uncle Thomas."

Dan touched the handle of a pistol at his waistband. "It might be an animal."

"Go look around."

Dan whirled on Luke, his eyes wide and his mouth agape. "But... "

"Go!"

Dan slowly made his way up the ladder and out of the kiva.

Maggie swallowed. "You're the one behind all these attacks?"

Luke switched his gaze to her, expression bland. "Yeah."

She leaned forward, clasping her bound hands together. "And our dad?"

Luke's expression darkened. "You're asking if I killed him? Yes. I killed him."

"Why? Even... if you're willing to kill me—I'm someone you barely know. But your own father? The man who raised you?"

He scowled, scooting closer to her. "Well, now, isn't that an exaggeration? Want to know why my mom left him, Maggie?" Luke snorted a laugh. "Dad was always caught up in you and your mother. He tried to move on, I guess, but he never could let go of the past. You have all those letters he wrote. That woman... your mother, never read a single one, but he kept sending them year after year. He never even met you, but he couldn't stop talking about his precious daughter." Luke's face contorted into an ugly mask.

He crouched and clamped her face in his hand, fingernails digging into her skin. "He wrote you letters. Every year. But he never even—he didn't care. Not about my mother. Not about me. I'd visit him in the summer, and we'd go on the obligatory outings, but we never had the close bond we should have. My mother knew how little invested he was in their marriage, and she split. Found someone better and left."

His eyes were like black holes boring into Maggie. "That wasn't justice. Not for everything he took from us. From me. To lose what he already didn't care for. There's nothing in that for me. The property his old mobile home sits on, though?" He sneered. "There're thousands of ways to repay me back on that land." He patted her face twice roughly then stood. "And I'm not letting you swoop in from nowhere and get between me and what I'm owed."

"So, all these recent overtures of getting closer—of building a relationship with me—that was all a lie? You never really wanted to have a sister?"

"Sorry, Maggie. I had to throw your pal Sergeant Yazzie off my trail. I had to put them on the scent of dear old Uncle Thomas. He's been a rebel his entire life." He shrugged. "At first, I figured on setting him up to take the fall for this. Now, I guess it'll be Dan. I can take care of him after you."

His dark eyes gleamed with malice in the shadowy light. Luke's boots crunched on the kiva's dirt floor as he paced. "You should have just sold that old rickety mobile home to me and gone on about your business, Maggie. Then none of this would have ever happened. But you had to get sentimental about the junk our old man left behind and spoil my plans."

She stared at him, tears streaming down her face. "How could I have been so wrong about you? I thought I could reach you. I thought you would want a sister as much as I longed for a brother."

Luke cradled her face with a gentleness that didn't belong. His thumb brushed her cheek, almost tender— almost real. Then his eyes went flat. The warmth drained from his face, replaced by something cold and dead.

He leaned in and kissed her forehead.

She didn't breathe.

"Time to grow up, sis. Fairytale's over."

Maggie jerked away and looked down at her wrists, blood seeping around the edge of the strong tape.

"I'm bleeding, Luke. Won't you take this tape off me? At least for a while? I'm starving and I need to… go outside."

He crouched in the firelight, an ominous glow illuminating his face. "Okay, I'll free your hands long enough to take care of business, then I'm binding you again." He sliced through the heavy tape with his pocketknife.

Maggie heaved a sigh of relief and rubbed her wrists. She gave him a questioning look and started for the ladder.

"Don't get any brave notions." Luke pulled a gun from his waistband and pointed it at her.

"Don't worry. I'm not feeling very brave right now."

Luke quirked a smile. "Sorry about your lack of privacy." He yelled toward the ladder. "Dan! She's coming up for a minute. Watch her."

She moved cautiously up the ladder and over the stone ledge. The late afternoon sun beamed through the canopy of trees, casting long, menacing shadows. She strained her ears. Dan Hoskie was out here somewhere, investigating the noise he'd heard. She sat still, her senses heightened to any sound. Her heart squeezed at the thought of Nathan. He'd move heaven and earth to find her. She didn't doubt that for one second.

Maggie crouched behind a bush and listened. There it was again. A rustling from down the path. Nearer to her, Dan crept through the underbrush, his gun drawn.

She heard another rustle, closer this time, and watched as Dan tightened his grip on his gun. He took a step forward, ready to strike. A figure lunged from the shadows and tackled him to the ground. From behind, someone grabbed Dan and hit him over the head with the butt of a gun. He lay unconscious.

Nathan looked up at Maggie and put a finger to his lips. "Shhhh… quiet."

~

Nathan shoved Dan onto his side and snatched up his gun. He cuffed Dan's hands behind him.

Thomas crept from the trees and approached Nathan.

Maggie threw her hands to her mouth, utter disbelief showing in her eyes.

"Nathan... Uncle Thomas." She whispered the words.

"Shhh... I'll explain everything later. Get back in the tree line." Nathan waved her away from the ladder.

The rustling of movement inside the kiva sent Maggie scurrying, and Nathan and Thomas moved closer to the entrance of the ceremonial pit.

"Dan... what's going on up there?" Luke's voice echoed from down below. "Dan!"

Footsteps clacking on the wooden ladder echoed through the still air. Nathan and Thomas scurried into the shadow of the trees that hid the ancient ruins.

Luke's head emerged from the entrance. He surveyed the area around the ruin. "Dan?"

Finally, he pulled himself fully out of the pit and crouched, scanning his surroundings and watching.

A wave of dizziness hit Maggie, and she swayed sideways, snapping a twig with her foot.

Luke lunged, springing on Maggie like a mountain lion after its prey. Before she could react, he pulled her to her feet and grasped her arm roughly.

"Where's Dan? There was a lot of movement out here. Don't lie to me."

"I—I don't know. I heard noises, too."

In the shadows, Dan rolled his head from side to side and mumbled. Luke drew his gun and edged carefully toward Dan.

Maggie's breath came in quick, shallow bursts. Cold sweat beaded on her face. Desperate to stop Luke as he inched closer to Dan, she whispered a prayer, summoned every ounce of her strength, and lunged forward. She spun and raised one foot to waist level with all her might. Her kick landed hard. Luke's pistol flew from his grip. It spiraled through the air, then landed on the ground with a loud *thud*.

Nathan burst from the shadows, diving for the gun.

Luke dove for the gun. Nathan tackled him. They crashed to the ground, grappling for control.

Nathan stretched his arm. Just reaching the pistol, he clenched it in his fist. He grunted as Luke's elbow slammed into his ribs. He countered with a punch. Luke arched back with the blow, but the gun went flying again, higher this time.

Maggie's eyes followed it as it arced above them. Without thinking, she bolted forward, reaching out to grab it as it fell to the ground.

Before her fingers could close around it, the revolver hit the earth with a thud.

A shot rang out.

She stretched her hand to the gun, then lay motionless.

~

Silence fell. Then chaos.

Nathan froze, then dove for the gun. He snatched it, then pointed it at Luke as he knelt over Maggie.

"Maggie! Are you okay?" He turned her over gently and caressed her cheek.

Her eyes fluttered open, and she drew her face into a grimace.

Horror surged through Nathan as he watched a crimson blood stain blossom on her white blouse at the shoulder.

"Oh, no... no," he whispered and bent down to her.

Thomas rushed to Maggie's side and took her hand. "Hold on, *atsi'*. You'll be okay."

Nathan pressed the button on his shirt mic to call dispatch. Nothing... no reception. He pulled his cell from his pocket and found he had no bars.

Leaves rustled from behind the tree where Dan lay handcuffed. Nathan waved the pistol at Luke.

"Get over there next to your friend, Dan."

Luke's jaw tightened as he looked at his injured sister. His voice was low, steady. "You think this means you've won. It doesn't. You'll never be one of us."

Maggie turned her head and tears rolled down her cheeks.

Thomas grasped Maggie's hand. He turned on Luke, his words full of rancor. "You're wrong, Luke. She's my brother's daughter. She is one of us." He pulled off his jacket and pressed it over her bleeding shoulder, applying pressure to the wound.

She arched up, a harsh breath escaping her clenched teeth, then fell back, gasping.

Thomas hovered over her, a deep groove forming between his brows. "I'm sorry, Maggie. I've got to staunch the bleeding."

He turned to Nathan. "We need to get her out of here."

"Yes, emergency services are on the way. They should be here soon." *I hope.*

"White medicine—"

Nathan raised his voice to talk over Thomas. "Is what will keep her alive."

The older man clenched his teeth and scowled, but didn't argue.

Nathan pulled the second set of handcuffs from his belt and secured Luke's right wrist to Dan's left.

He handed Thomas the keys to his truck. "Backup should be on the way. Go down and meet them. If they're not here in ten minutes, go for help." Thomas nodded and set off.

Nathan settled by Maggie and swept a stray strand of hair from her face. "Hang on. We'll get you to the hospital soon." He shook his head. "I'm so sorry."

Her head lolled to the side to meet his eyes. "Sorry?"

His hand lingered on her cheek. "Yes, sorry about all of this."

"You have nothing to apologize for."

"I let you get injured... Never should have left you alone, even at my family's home. I thought you'd be safe there..."

She grasped his hand, her fingers trembling violently. "You found me, didn't you? I knew you would. I never doubted it. I don't want to think about what would have happened to me if you hadn't."

Nathan swallowed hard, trying to keep his emotions in check. "If I were a better cop—"

"Stop." She narrowed her eyes at him. "Don't even go there. You did everything right. You were amazing." Her hand trembled in his. "You're a super cop. Imagine where you'll be when you're your uncle's age."

He chuckled softly, taking her hand between both of his. "Okay, you win. You're as stubborn as ever."

"Yeah, guess I am." She cringed and threw a hand to her shoulder. "It seems to be an Adakai trait."

Federal agents, led by Elise Martin, rushed forward. Yoyetewa and NNPD followed behind with EMTs and their medical equipment. Nathan backed away from Maggie to allow them to begin their work, starting the IV and stabilizing her. They moved her onto a stretcher.

Nathan pulled out his cell phone, staring at the screen. He scrolled through his contacts, stopping with the name Uncle Ben highlighted. His finger paused, just shy of pressing it. He needed to give an update. He'd found Maggie, and she was alive.

The EMTs lifted her stretcher. One of them called to him. "Are you riding with us?"

Chapter Twelve

Maggie opened her eyes to white walls, white sheets, and the scent of cleaning chemicals. *Oh, boy, not again.*

The hospital. This was the second time in as many weeks Maggie had woken to find herself in a hospital bed. First, after she'd skinned her arm so deeply. Now the shoulder wound. Her memory replayed the scenes in the kiva. Of Luke, Nathan's rescue, and the ride in the ambulance after the gunshot. *Right. That's why I'm here this time.*

She shifted her shoulder slightly, testing it. Her eyes slammed closed, and she hissed through the pain.

The door opened with a small creak, and her eyes darted to it. Her pulse sped up. No, Nathan had arrested Luke and Dan. She was safe, right? *God, please keep me safe.*

She released her breath. "Mom."

Her mother slipped quietly into the room. Blonde, blue eyed, and looking only half her age. Of course, Mom would never look her age, but now her eyes had a few worry lines around them.

"Maggie, honey."

"Mom. What a surprise. What are you doing here?"

"The lieutenant from the local police station called and said you were wounded." Jaqueline sat on the edge of the bed and placed a box on Maggie's lap. "Your favorite chocolates." She smiled. "I rushed here as quickly as I could. I had to make sure that my baby was okay." She grabbed Maggie's hand and held it between both of her pale, perfectly manicured ones. "The doctor says you'll be okay, that the bullet went through cleanly, so it'll heal well." She tipped her head to one side, her bob falling to frame her concerned face. "But how do you feel?"

Maggie shrugged on instinct, then stopped to grit her teeth. "Not great. I mean, probably better than many people feel after being shot, but—" She laughed. "Not very good."

"Of course. Not only the bullet wound, but learning everything about your father, your brother—" Jackie stopped. "You've lived a nightmare since you got here. I wish you could've talked to me…"

"I wish I could've, too."

"They said John was probably poisoned." Her face tightened. "Probably? Couldn't they exhume his remains, test for poisons, and give everyone closure about that?"

Maggie shook her head. "No. I asked about that, too. Dad was cremated, so no. But a big jar of olives from his refrigerator tested positive for arsenic, so they know how it happened. Luke gave him the olives and poisoned him. He even admitted it. Then he tried to murder me and frame his own uncle. Hard to believe, isn't it?"

Maggie stopped and searched her mother's face. "But last time we talked, we argued. And I know how much you *hate being on the reservation*, so why come here?"

Her mother flinched at the sarcastic remark. "Honey, if you think I haven't spent every second since that phone call haunted by the mistakes I've made in the last twenty-five years—about you and your dad, you're wrong. I did love John. When we married, I was a young girl living in a fantasy world." She looked down. "Yes, I should have read John's letters. Even if we weren't together, I should have let him visit you. I should have told you about him."

She shook her head. "I own up to my mistakes, Maggie. I'm sorry. The way I cut John out of your life and lied to you. It was all wrong, and I can't fix it now. I was just so afraid of going off-script. I had this plan in my mind about how my life should go. Finish school, marry a successful man, have a brilliant career in the city. And for the most part, I've done that. But it's become all too clear how many people I've hurt while forging that life for myself."

She met Maggie's eyes. "I can't fix it, but I promise you—from this day forward, I will never lie to you or take you for granted. Never take anyone for granted. I swear it."

Maggie sniffed back tears. "Mom..."

"Can you ever forgive me?"

Maggie nodded, tears slipping free. "Yes, I forgive you, Mom."

Her mother leaned in, capturing Maggie in a careful hug. Maggie returned it, grateful in her pain and the aftermath of her nightmare, to feel her mother's arms around her. She buried her face into her mom's shoulder, the box of chocolates crumpling on the bed between them.

Her mom leaned back and dabbed her flawlessly made-up eyes with a tissue. "I'm going to do better. Starting with taking care of you. Your shoulder—and your injured arm—I'm going to stay with you while you recover, even after you go home to Albuquerque. Breakfast in bed and homemade chicken soup." She squeezed Maggie's hand. "Don't worry about a thing."

Maggie's smile felt brittle. The weight of this enormous decision dragged on her. She wanted to stay here, and she knew she was in love with Nathan. But she had no prospects for employment here. More, she'd worked hard for her position at the university, and she loved her job.

"Yeah. The dig fell apart, and there's no way I can work like this, anyway. I guess I'll have to go back to Albuquerque." Why did that make her stomach sink like a stone?

~

Maggie reluctantly lifted a square of translucent red gelatin on her spoon. She frowned, brought it to her mouth, then dropped it back into the little beige bowl. The food was still as bad as she remembered.

Voices droned from the TV with a mid-morning soap opera. Maggie sighed.

The door to her room opened, and Maggie gladly switched her attention. Nathan.

He stood in the door, looking handsome in his

faded jeans, denim shirt, and western boots. He held a bouquet of red and orange zinnias. She clicked off the TV.

"Hey."

"Hey, yourself. Come in."

He crossed the room, grabbed the pink plastic water pitcher from her tray for the flowers and sat them on her bedside table. He settled into a visitor's chair by the bed. "How are you feeling today?"

She looked up at the ceiling. "Ummm... about as well as can be expected, I guess." Her eyes darted to the flowers. Her favorites. He'd remembered. "Thank you for the Zinnias."

He shrugged. "I thought I heard you say you like these." He reached out and laid his open hand on the bed at her side.

She placed her hand in his, and he squeezed it.

"So, how are you really feeling? You've been through so much in the last few weeks."

"I'm doing okay. Really. The doc says I'll be fine." She glanced up at the bag of antibiotics that dripped into her other hand. "He's taking precautions against infection."

Nathan looked down and shook his head. "It's just inconceivable, the things Luke did. I can't wrap my brain around it."

She felt her eyes well up with tears. "Neither can I."

He leaned forward. "Aw, Maggie, I'm sorry. I didn't mean to make you feel worse."

"You didn't. But I don't think I'll ever comprehend the hatred Luke harbored in his heart. I would have loved it if we could have been real family to each other."

"I know." Nathan stroked her hand. "Oh, speaking of family, you may have lost a brother, but you've gained an uncle. Thomas hasn't stopped talking about his "atsi' Maggie" since this happened. You've won him over. The man's crazy about you."

She laughed with delight, then stopped short. "Oh, don't make me laugh again. That makes everything hurt."

He chuckled. "Yes, ma'am. Sorry." He pressed a quick kiss on her hand. "On the topic of your fan club—my mother asked me to tell you she's praying that you heal quickly."

A rush of warmth flooded Maggie. "Nathan, thank her for me. I've felt God's hand on me throughout this entire ordeal. Really, since the moment your mother first mentioned the Jesus Road to me, and I read my dad's first letter to my mother, I've felt something happening inside me."

A slow smile spread over Nathan's face. "This sounds like an answer to many prayers."

Nathan's smile was sunshine bringing light and warmth to the bleak hospital room. He brought the back of her hand to his lips and laid a gentle kiss on it. "This makes me happier than I can say." He leaned in to Maggie and paused, as if asking permission to kiss her. She lifted her head and touched her lips to his.

He stroked her cheek. "Maggie, you know how I feel about you, don't you?"

"I think so."

He settled his intense, dark eyes on her. "It might seem sudden, but my feelings have been building since the day we met. You knocked me off my feet with your beauty, and I've watched as you proved to be just as beautiful on the inside." He gently kissed her cheek. "I love you."

Maggie smiled and planted another tiny peck on his lips. "And I feel the same way, Nathan." She turned her head and focused on the bare white wall.

He froze. "Is there a 'but'?" His tone was cautious, as if bracing for a blow he hadn't seen coming.

"Kind of. I mean... yeah. There is." She looked at him. "My mother was just here before you came in. She plans to stay with me at my dad's mobile home while I recover. Then maybe at the apartment in Albuquerque for a while afterwards. Not that it's a problem for you and me, but I'm feeling a little confused and conflicted about things."

She blew out a frustrated breath. "I've been telling you from the beginning that I want to stay in Chinle. That I want to stay on my dad's property and wake every morning to the Lukachukais out my back door."

Nathan nodded. "So far, I'm not hearing a problem."

"Well, when I get out of here, I'll have some recovery time, and there'll be therapy to regain full use of my arm after these injuries. And of course, I won't go back to work at Canyon de Chelly."

He nodded again, a deep groove forming between his eyes.

"I don't know of any job opportunities around here that match my qualifications. There are just so many roadblocks."

Nathan's face went blank, then confused. "None of this sounds like a problem we can't figure out. You could come stay at our place after you're released from the hospital. Or, since we've locked up Luke and Dan, you and your mother could stay at your mobile home, if you'd like that better. You could worry about finding a new job a little further down the line."

Maggie sighed and looked down. "I'm... just feeling a little confused about my future—I mean, I'm not even the person I grew up believing I was. I don't know exactly what I want to do with my life right now.

"One thing I'm sure of, though, is that I'm going to explore my faith. I've always been a believer, but now I'm feeling compelled to learn more. To really walk the walk."

"So... you need space, then?"

She shook her head. "Not exactly. But maybe for now. Just for a while, until I get things figured out."

He laid her hand back on the blanket and kissed her cheek again. "Okay, Maggie Adakai. I can do that." He stood up and walked toward the door, then turned back to her, his face a mask of turmoil and sadness. "I'll keep you updated on the case. There are still a few loose ends to tie up."

She pasted on a smile and nodded.

The door clicked closed, leaving the room empty and silent. Maggie turned her gaze toward the window. The wind scattered the desert dust, and something in her shifted with it.

Tears slipped free and rolled down her face. Maggie eased an arm around her side, hugging herself as she swiped her cheeks. She wanted to call him back, but how could she? She needed time—to get her heart and mind in order before joining her life to someone else's.

Nathan's exit left her feeling cold and dead inside.

Maybe she'd just thrown away the best thing that had ever come her way. Maybe she'd just lost the love of her life.

~

Nathan tramped out of the hospital, stride forceful. Shell-shocked, he barely saw the world around him as he made his way across the parking lot. He opened the door to his truck and climbed inside.

What had he expected from Maggie when he told her he loved her? Certainly not what he got. Not for her to ask him to back off and tell him she'd probably return to Albuquerque. He stared out the windshield at nothing, his breath coming in shallow bursts. He told himself she needed space. Not everything needed to be solved today

His phone chimed, and he looked at the name on the screen. Uncle Ben. *I think I'll let this one go to voicemail.*

But it could be something work-related. He swiped the phone to answer.

"Hi, Uncle Ben."

"Hey, Nathan. Are you coming home anytime soon?"

Nathan sighed. "Actually, I'm off today. I'm thinking I need to go to my apartment and spend a couple days there. It's been badly neglected lately, and I have a hundred things to do. Could you tell Mom for me?"

Silence.

"Uncle Ben?"

"Would you come by your mom's place first? We

need to talk."

"Is there something new with the case?"

"No, it isn't that." Uncle Ben kept his speech slow and steady. "We should talk. It won't take long. Just stop by the house, will you?

Nathan let out a resigned sigh. "Okay. I'll be there soon." He started the engine and slipped it into gear. *This day is not going the way I planned at all.*

~

A red dust cloud trailed Nathan's car down the long drive, announcing his arrival. He parked in his usual spot under a tree and climbed out of his truck. Barely glancing at the house, he took his time reaching the front porch, where Uncle Ben waited for him.

He stood up and handed Nathan a glass of iced tea. "Come on. Let's go out to the hogan."

Surprise surged through Nathan. He said nothing, but followed Uncle Ben the short distance to the earthen structure.

Uncle Ben stopped beside the door. "Let's not go inside. Let's go out back. I want to see the mesas."

He led Nathan to the rear of the hogan and pulled two plastic outdoor chairs into a shady spot. "I like these because they rock." He plopped down into one of them.

Nathan did the same and took a sip of his iced tea. He rocked back and crossed an ankle over his knee, his eyes fixed on the distant mesas. "This was a good idea. I always love this view." He pointed to the middle mesa. "Look—I think that's a golden eagle circling."

"Yes, I've seen it there before. I'd bet that's a

mama eagle with a nest on that mesa. I've seen them there and watched with binoculars. They seem to like it. That appears to be a favorite nesting spot."

"Huh. I'll bet you're right." Nathan turned back to his uncle and noticed he wasn't in uniform, as he usually was. Today, he wore an old pair of brown pants and a western shirt with mother-of-pearl snaps down the front and on the pockets. Each pocket flap bore intricate embroidery that he knew Aunt Shirley had applied for him. Uncle Ben always seemed so different when he dressed this way.

Nathan took another swallow of tea. "What did you want to talk about? You said it isn't about the Adakai case."

"No, it's not work related." He gazed off into the distance and rocked. "I was thinking about when your father died. It was a very hard time for your mother. That's when your Aunt Shirley and I moved here to help her."

"Yes, I remember that. I was only eleven years old." He wrinkled his forehead and stared into the distance.

"You probably didn't know this, but I was always so jealous of your father. He was very traditional, much like Thomas. But highly respected in our community. I know some expected him to become a *hataalii*—a medicine man—when he was a boy." Uncle Ben stole a glance at Nathan. "People came to him for advice and help with their ceremonies. I admired him more than anyone I knew."

"Yes, he could have been a healer, but my mother chose the Christian path, and Dad wouldn't go against her. She raised us boys the same way. I'm grateful for that."

An evening breeze blew across them and the sun blazed on the mesas.

Uncle Ben sat quietly rocking. Nathan knew it would take him a while to get to the point. It was the Navajo way, and Nathan wouldn't push him with questions. They rocked and watched as clouds drifted over the Lukachukais, creating strange shadows on the mesas.

"When my children grew up, I hoped one of them would follow me into law enforcement, but neither of my sons was interested. Both your cousins became engineers. And I'm very proud of them both. They've made good lives for themselves." He gave Nathan a sidelong glance. "But it was you, Nephew, who followed me. And I couldn't be prouder of you if you were my own son."

Nathan felt his eyes go wide. "But Uncle Ben. I could never live up to your reputation. You're a hard act to follow."

Uncle Ben shot a severe glance at Nathan. "Don't say that. Don't even think such a thing. You've become a first-rate police officer. I fully expect to see you behind my desk someday. You've got it in you. All you need is the years of experience under your belt."

Nathan shook his head. "I've made a couple of blunders lately that make me wonder if I really am cut out for this job."

"Nathan, you're twenty-seven years old. You wouldn't believe some of my mistakes in the early days. I once arrested a drunk and didn't secure him properly. He escaped and got back on the road, killed a woman before the night was over." He turned away. "I still have to live with that every day."

Nathan straightened in his chair and put his feet on the ground. "Uncle Ben, I'd have never imagined you making rookie errors."

"Well, I don't even have the excuse of being a rookie at the time. I was young, and I made a big mistake. Mistakes are a part of maturing." Uncle Ben turned and looked Nathan in the eyes. "You're a good cop, and you'll be even better as time goes by. I've been tough on you because I want you to be the best. I want to give you the benefit of my years of experience. Not every man has that available to them."

"I think I should be doing everything right by this time."

Uncle Ben's tone was stern. "Nobody does everything right. You hold yourself to an impossible standard. Once a mistake is made, learn from it, then let it go. If you keep this attitude, you'll end up with ulcers."

Nathan felt something inside himself relax. The tension he'd carried on his shoulders melted with those words. He leaned back and lifted his eyes to the wide-open sky. *So, Uncle Ben thinks I'll be behind his desk someday.*

And after all these years, Uncle Ben said he was proud of him. The words freed him.

"You're a super cop. Imagine where you'll be when you're your uncle's age." Maggie had said this to him. Her image flashed in his mind, and his good mood dissolved as quickly as it had come. A future without Maggie was something he didn't want to think about.

Uncle Ben turned to him. A frown tugged at his weathered face. "Okay, what else is bothering you? It's that girl, isn't it? What happened today?"

"Yeah. Something did happen." He shook his head. "It's crazy. Ever since she came here, I've tried to keep her away from that mobile home. Now that Luke and Dan are no threat, and she could stay there if she wants to, she's talking about going back to Albuquerque. What's wrong with women?"

"Maybe you need to give her some time. Life has turned her upside down and inside out lately. She probably needs to get stabilized before she can think about her future."

"That's pretty much what she told me today."

"Then listen. If it's meant to be, things will turn out okay for you."

Nathan smiled at the older man. "I'm glad we talked, Uncle. You've shared a lot of wisdom with me today."

Uncle Ben's phone buzzed, and he answered. Nathan watched his face pale.

"Okay, thanks for letting me know. I'll get this taken care of immediately."

"What is it? What's happened."

Uncle Ben turned to Nathan. "I don't know how, but Luke made bail. He's out of jail right now."

Chapter Thirteen

Nathan jogged down the hallway of the Chinle hospital, shoved his way through the double doors, and slid to a stop at Maggie's room, hand on his Glock. He pushed her door open and stood at the threshold, his hand still on his weapon. Afterward, he visually searched every corner of the room, then opened the bathroom door.

Maggie looked up, her eyes wide with surprise. "Nathan, you came back." She scooted up in bed and chuffed a short laugh when he opened the bathroom. "What in the world is going on?"

Nathan came to her bedside. "Luke's out of jail. Somehow, he made bail. He's on the streets."

Maggie's jaw dropped. "Seriously? How can that be? He's been living in that rundown duplex and driving an old car. Where could he get enough money for bail?"

Nathan dropped into the chair next to her bed. "That's what I've been thinking about as I drove over here. I see this as proof that Luke's been selling looted artifacts. He must have been squirreling away money all this time, and that's how he was able to pay bail."

She nodded. "That makes sense." She rubbed goosebumps from her arm. "Thank you for coming back, Nathan." She smiled at him, her eyes both grateful and hesitant. "I was afraid I'd never see you again."

He reached out a hand to her and leaned in closer. "Maggie, I told you I love you, and nothing you say or do is going to change that. If you need time to adjust to so many changes, I'll give you that time."

The door burst open, and Nathan jumped to his feet. Merv stood in the doorway in a crouching position, gun drawn.

As soon as he saw Nathan, he straightened, lowered his Glock, and sighed. "I heard about Luke and thought he was in the room." He entered and closed the door behind himself. "I'm happy to see we made it here first, Sergeant."

He smiled at Maggie. "How are you feeling? You've been through the mill lately."

Maggie returned his smile and adjusted the flowered cotton hospital gown hanging halfway off her shoulder. "I'm doing okay, Merv, thank you." She sighed. "You're right, I have been through the mill and feel it, too. But the doctors say I'm going to be fine. There's just going to be a little recovery time."

"That's great to hear, ma'am. Sergeant Yazzie said you were so impressive at the kiva. We probably wouldn't have captured Luke if it weren't for you." A sudden blush spread over his face, and he looked at Nathan.

"Merv, you should grab a chair and station yourself outside the door." Nathan jerked his head toward the doorway.

"Yes, Sergeant." He grabbed the extra chair in the room and pulled it into the hallway.

Maggie chuckled and turned to Nathan. "You know, I really like Merv. He's come to feel like a friend to me."

Nathan looked down. "Yeah. I like him, too, but I can't let up on him during his training. I want him to be a good police officer, and that means I stay on his back." He shrugged. "Actually, Merv's been doing well in his training. He proved himself on the mountain, and I'll tell him that when the time's right."

He shrugged. "I had a great talk with Uncle Ben today. He opened my eyes to a few things, and he made me realize I may have been a little tougher than necessary on Merv. I've had overly high expectations of myself, and I probably transferred some of that onto him."

Maggie raised an eyebrow. "Oh, Nathan. I'm so happy to hear you say that. I mean, not about you being tough on Merv, but that you and your uncle talked. It sounds like you did some real self-reflection." She touched his arm. "You needed that. It's true, you've been hard on yourself, when I've known all along that you're a first-rate police officer. You've always gone above and beyond for me."

A small smile stretched his lips. "Well... thank you. But I might have been a little more motivated in your case."

Nathan's phone rang, and Detective Deschene's voice filtered through. "Yes, Detective, Yoyetewa and I are both here. We're taking the first shift guarding Maggie until she's released from the hospital."

"Okay, that's fine, but I'm thinking we should set

up another trap for Adakai. If he sees Yoyetewa by her door, he'll run. I mean, true, it'll keep Miss Beaumont safe, but if he tries something, we want to catch the guy, don't we?"

"Sure, I just don't want to put her in danger."

Maggie snapped to attention. "What? What does he want?"

Nathan blew out an exasperated breath. "Detective, I'm putting you on speakerphone."

"Yes, Miss Beaumont. We think we've got a way to trap Adakai. If he tries again, we'll be ready. If he makes another attempt on your life, we can arrest him. Otherwise, he'll run, and you'll be right back where you were—constantly looking over your shoulder."

Maggie gazed toward the door, a solemn look in her eyes. She nodded. "Yes. I guess you're right. What did you have in mind?"

"Well, it's evening now, anyway, so I think something as simple as pulling Yoyetewa out of there, turning out the lights and positioning Sergeant Yazzie in a dark corner of the room would do the trick. We could station Yoyetewa with Miss Beaumont's mother at the mobile home. If, or rather, when, Adakai comes into her room, he'll be there waiting." Deschene's voice trailed off. "Of course, there'll still be an element of danger for you, Miss Beaumont."

Nathan paused. "Don't you think Luke will smell a trap? Why wouldn't we have a guard at her door? We did for Sarah Nez while she was here."

"I thought about that but, from what I know of him, I think Adakai's anger and desire to get revenge on Miss Beaumont will overpower his common sense. At least, I think it's worth the risk."

Nathan met Maggie's eyes. "I think it's the best way of handling this. Are you okay with it?"

Maggie nodded. "Yes, let's do it."

~

Nathan repositioned himself in the vinyl-covered recliner in the dim corner of the room. Maggie popped a barbeque flavored potato chip into her mouth and whispered to him. "Do you want one? You must be starving." She turned down the volume on The Wheel of Fortune.

"No, thanks. You know those things are terrible for you."

She turned, narrowed her eyes at him, and loudly crunched another chip.

"Aunt Shirley texted me. She and Uncle Ben are on their way here to visit you, and they're going to smuggle a cheeseburger and some onion rings in to me."

She turned to him again, her eyebrows raised and eyes wide. "Oh, and that's good for you, huh?"

"Well, maybe not, but it sure does taste good." His stomach rumbled at the thought of it.

"Well, my tray of gruel should be here soon. I'll share it with you, if you want me to."

"Hmm. No thanks."

The door creaked and Nathan put a hand on the Glock he had resting on the side table.

Aunt Shirley's silver-streaked head appeared around the edge of the door, then the rest of her body. "Don't shoot. I have food for you." She laughed and entered the room, a large gift bag at her side bearing the words *Get Well Soon* in bright colors.

"Man, I can smell that already." Nathan straightened and rubbed his hands together. Uncle Ben followed his wife into the room. He was still wearing the western shirt he'd worn that morning. It struck Nathan again, how he seemed like a different man when in civilian clothes.

Shirley set the large bag on the end of the bed and unpacked it. First Nathan's burger and onion rings, and then a smaller gift bag.

"Maggie, this is just a little something for you from Ben and I, and also from Wanda."

Maggie's mouth dropped open. "Oh, thank you so much. You didn't need to do that."

"But we wanted to."

Nathan scooted to the edge of his chair, watching to see what his family brought for Maggie.

Shirley handed the gift bag to Maggie. She pulled back the yellow tissue paper and drew out a small white box. Her hands trembled slightly as she removed the lid. Maggie gasped and lifted out a pair of beautiful turquoise earrings.

"Shirley, these are exquisite!" She held them up and showed them to Nathan. "I don't know what to say. These match perfectly with the necklace my father made. This is beyond amazing."

Shirley touched her on her arm. "Wanda and I talked about it and we want you to have them. They're very old. Not made by your father, but an older artist from our town." She laughed lightly. "You need them to go with the necklace."

Maggie looked up at the older woman and held out her uninjured arm to take her in an embrace. "Thank you so very much. And tell Wanda I love them more than any gift I've ever received."

"I'll tell her."

Nathan shot a glance at Uncle Ben and he lifted the corners of his mouth in a knowing smile. Clearly, the rest of his family loved Maggie, too. Parting with these vintage earrings was not something done lightly by his mother and aunt.

Maggie cleared her throat and frowned down at her tray. She turned to Nathan. "Well, you'd better dig into that cheeseburger before you starve." She laughed. "And could I have one of those onion rings? They smell delicious."

Uncle Ben updated Nathan and Maggie on the investigation while Nathan finished his meal. He wadded up the bag and tossed it into the trash can. Maggie grimaced and shoved her dinner tray away.

"Officer Tsosie will be here to take over your shift tomorrow morning, if we don't catch Luke Adakai in our little trap tonight. And Miss Beaumont, we've cleared your mobile home. It's no longer a crime scene, so you can do as you please with it. Nathan mentioned that you might want to move into it."

She looked down at her hands. "Yes, I'd thought about it but now I'm not sure. I have a lot of thinking to do. My head's spinning from everything that's happened in my life over the past few weeks. My mother's in town, so I know I'll be staying in the mobile home while I recover. She's getting it stocked and cleaned right now. If I know my mom, it'll look like a new place when I get there."

"That's more than understandable. Take your time. You want to be sure before you make any big changes."

He looked over at Shirley and patted her hand. "Well, we'd better get out of here and let this girl get some rest."

"Yes, you're right." Aunt Shirley looked at Maggie. "And if you decide you want to stay on the reservation, Ben and I just might know of a career opportunity that would match your background and education."

Maggie looked up, startled. Her eyes went wide and lit up with a momentary excitement. "Really? Something close by?"

"Maybe. We'll talk about it soon."

"Alright. Goodnight, Mr. and Mrs. Benally. Please give Wanda my regards and thank her for the earrings."

~

The evening shift nurse slipped into Maggie's room, her shoes silent on the tiled floor. She erased the name of the day shift RN from the dry erase board and replaced it with her own. "How are you feeling tonight, Miss Beaumont?" She moved to Maggie's bedside and checked her vitals.

"Here's your pain medication. You'll sleep like a baby now." With a smooth, deliberate motion, she inserted the syringe into the IV port and slowly pushed the plunger.

Maggie smiled up at her. "Thank you, Tammy. I was starting to feel a little uncomfortable."

Tammy patted her arm. "Rest well. Use your buzzer if you need anything."

Maggie turned her head for a reassuring look at Nathan. Yes, he was still there. Still looking out for her safety, just as he always had.

"What do you want to watch, Nathan? I think there's a good classic movie about to start."

"Whatever you decide is fine with me. Besides, you'll be asleep in ten minutes, then I'll turn on the baseball game."

She threw a paper cup at him.

They settled in and a horror movie host introduced the monster movie. Only the flicker of blue light from the television illuminated the hospital room as the amphibian creature stalked its prey through the murky water.

She barely caught Nathan muttering to himself. "You asleep? Maggie, I'll be right back." His voice faded as his footsteps moved away from her. Maggie mumbled something, then her breathing became steady. She nuzzled her cheek into the pillow.

She was on the verge of deep sleep when an odd, scraping noise pulled her back. Maggie stirred, too sleepy to care.

Something buzzed under her skin, the sensation of someone next to her. Her eyes fluttered open, blinking repeatedly, adjusting to the blurry image before her. Luke. How was it possible? *This must be a nightmare.*

His face loomed only inches from hers. "Maggie... Sis," he whispered.

He raised up and stood over her, a pillow clasped in his hands. He stared down at her with a menacing smile.

Her stomach twisted in terror as she tried to move, but her limbs felt sluggish, trapped in a fog of confusion.

In one swift motion, he brought the pillow down

over her face. Maggie cried out, her voice a muffled distortion beneath the pillow. Panic seized her. She thrashed wildly in her bed to dislodge the pillow but the IV that tethered her to a pole hindered her attempts.

Luke shushed her, pressing the pillow harder. Maggie's throat clenched and she fought to scream.

A harsh whisper. "Quiet, now."

She heard a voice from the direction of the bathroom and a door slammed. "Maggie?"

Nathan! If only she could call out to him.

The pillow slipped and she gasped for air. She shoved it away, as a crash came from beside her.

In a blur of motion, Nathan tackled Luke to the floor, the two men smashing into the bedside table, sending it, and everything on it, flying.

Luke fought like a man possessed, kicking out wildly as Nathan grappled with him. He knocked Nathan's head into the wall, then snatched up a vase of flowers, slamming it into Nathan's head.

Nathan let out a hoarse groan and staggered under the blow.

"No!" Maggie launched herself at Luke. She screamed as her IV stand jerked her back, the needle ripping free. Clutching her arm, she fought the pain and snatched up the IV stand. With all her strength, she swung it. The metal rod struck Luke across the shoulders, sending him sprawling to the floor. Nathan lunged at Luke and pinned him to the floor, then twisted his arms behind his back.

"Luke Adakai, you are under arrest. You have the right to remain silent…"

As Nathan secured Luke and read him his rights, Maggie slumped back onto the bed, pressing a hand to her bleeding arm. She shivered as the weight of what had just happened washed over her.

Luke, disabled on the floor, glared at her with pure hatred, spitting curses under his breath, but Maggie could feel nothing but a hollow ache in her chest as she looked at him—her brother, her flesh and blood.

Luke wrenched his arms and tried to break free. "You can't arrest me. I won't go to jail. I'd rather die! This is all your fault, you half-blood—"

Nathan jerked Luke to his feet, his face tight with determination.

The door burst open and hospital security flew into the room, taking Luke into custody.

She pictured her dad's Bible, the words highlighted, *"even as Christ forgave you, so you also must do."*

Maggie shouted out to Luke as officers led him through the door. Her voice broke and tears streamed down her face. "Luke, I know you're angry. And you've hurt me in every way you could. But you're my brother...my flesh and blood. I love you and I'll always love you. I wanted you in my life. Never forget that."

~

Maggie winced as she adjusted the sling on her arm and hefted her bag of belongings in her good hand.

"Let me get that." Nathan took her bag and steadied her by the arm. "You sure you're good to go home?"

"Yeah. I'm more than ready to get out of here."

He wheeled her down the hallway, out of the lobby, and to his pickup that waited outside the double doors.

He opened her door for her, pushed her wheel chair back inside then climbed in himself. They drove in silence, neither able to put into words the impact of the past twenty-four hours.

"Well, this time you're home free. No way is Luke getting out of this one. He'll be behind bars for the rest of his life. You can finally rest easy."

Maggie nodded. "Yeah. It's almost unreal that this is all behind me. That it's finished. Terri called me this morning, and we had a long talk about a lot of things. I feel like I let her and the team down. She's been my best friend through thick and thin."

"It's not like you won't see her now that you're not on the dig."

"Yes, I'm sure we'll find ways to stay in touch."

"I'm sure you will. He touched her hand. "My mother boxed up all the things you had at her place. It's in the back of the truck."

"Thank her for me. All your family have been wonderful, and you, of course."

Nathan shrugged. "You're a hard one not to like." She turned and took in his strong, handsome profile, but he wouldn't look at her. Had she ruined things? How long would there be an awkwardness between the two of them? How did she want to handle it? It had been a long time since Maggie hadn't known her own mind.

The truck turned down the access road to her father's mobile home—her mobile home, if she wanted it to be. "Thank you, Nathan. You've been everything I didn't know to hope for through all of this."

He dropped one of his hands from the wheel and squeezed hers. "You know it was no hardship."

The silence was less awkward as they pulled up to the mobile home. It hit her like a thunder bolt, that it felt like she was home. Even the outside of the trailer bore marks of her mother's sprucing. A new welcome mat and a pot with flowers sat out front. Jimmy ran barking to meet the truck, his tail wagging.

When Nathan came around and opened her door, she stepped out of the truck to meet him. "Hey, boy. I missed you too." She scratched behind his ears.

Her mother smiled and held the door open. "Maggie, so good to see you home, honey." She turned to Nathan. "And you must be Officer Yazzie?"

He stepped forward and offered a hand. "Yes, ma'am. Nathan Yazzie."

She shook it. "Jaqueline Beaumont. And aren't we grateful for you?" She gestured to the freshly shined side-table in front of new teal curtains by the window. "If you could just sit Maggie's things over here, I'll make sure they get put away."

Nathan nodded. "Yes, ma'am."

He helped Maggie into her father's comfortably worn Naugahyde recliner, then pushed his empty hands into his pockets, shoulders tense. Maggie looked up at him. "Thank you."

He gave a small smile. "Anytime."

He blew out a sigh and looked from Maggie to her mother. "Well, I guess I'll... see you soon. I'm sure I'll need to tie up a few loose threads on this case."

She reached out a hand to him and he leaned down to peck a small kiss on her cheek. "Yes, see you soon."

Chapter Fourteen

Maggie gave a soft groan as she settled back into the seat of Uncle Thomas' SUV. She eased the seatbelt around her injured arm and clicked it into place. She turned to him with a smile. "Thank you for driving me out to Canyon de Chelly. Mom could have done it later."

Uncle Thomas shrugged, a hint of a smile on his face. "I wanted the excuse to see you."

Maggie laughed. "Yeah, I must admit, I've been going nuts the last few days. All Mom's let me do is lay in bed eating chicken noodle soup."

"Good." Uncle Thomas turned down the classic country music drifting from the radio. She watched the mesas pass through the tinted windows, then rolled hers down for fresh air. Sagebrush and hot sand. *I can never get enough of that smell.*

The drive to Canyon de Chelly went quickly, as Uncle Thomas chatted comfortably with her. What a difference a few days could make. He was so different from the angry man she'd met at the sheep shearing.

He glanced at her quickly from the corner of his eyes. "Maggie, I want to be here for you. I know I can't replace the father you lost before you ever got to know him. But I can be the next best thing. We're blood family, you and me. I'll be here for you in any way you need me. I'm only going back to Flagstaff to clean out my apartment. Wanda has offered to let me stay with her family until I can get settled here in Chinle. This is home, and I'm ready to come back here and be a part of the community." He patted her hand. "Especially now that I have a new niece that needs me. I can teach you so many things about the Navajo culture."

Maggie beamed. "This is great! It's everything I'd hoped for. It's like half of me's been missing without Dad." She glanced down at her hands. "I only wish things could have turned out half as well with Luke. I think I'll have nightmares forever about my experience with him. It's very painful."

"It's painful for me, too, Atsi'. I tried to be family to Luke, but he was deeply wounded inside. I couldn't reach him. There was a darkness to him that I could never penetrate."

Uncle Thomas pulled up to Maggie's small trailer at Canyon de Chelly and she fished out her keys from her pocket. She didn't open the car door but gazed around the familiar camp site.

"Has it really only been a couple of weeks since I came here? And now I have to pack up all of my things and leave without finishing my job. The team has lost both Bruce and me. I feel like such a failure." She sighed. "You wouldn't believe how excited I was to work on this dig."

He turned off the ignition and spoke gently to her. "Still, good things came from it."

"Yeah. If it weren't for the dig, coming out here, I

may never have met you or Nathan's family."

"Or Nathan." He smiled.

The smile dropped from her face, and she turned away. "I haven't told you yet. I have to move back to Albuquerque. Leave you, the Yazzies, the reservation." She blinked rapidly. "I... I worry that once I do, this will all just feel like a dream. Like this side to my heritage, this side of my family that I discovered will just fall away."

He placed his large, weathered hand on her shoulder. "What? This isn't the strong willed, stubborn Maggie I know. What do you mean you have to go back to Albuquerque? You can do whatever you decide to do." He gently turned her face to look at him, and she leaned in to him.

She set her forehead on his shoulder and swallowed to clear her throat. "I don't know what to do, Uncle Thomas."

He ran a hand over her hair. "Atsi', can I be honest with you? You seem miserable. Do you really want to move back?"

She shook her head. "No. I don't. My heart is here. But I don't see any other way. I have to work." She leaned away and swiped at her face. She turned and stared out the window. "I have a career in Albuquerque. An apartment. I've made my life there. And everything...everything here has been amazing, but it's all been like a dream. A crazy dream."

"Everywhere is crazy, Maggie." Thomas shrugged. "You have a home here. Family. You have your dad's mobile home, and you'll be off work until you're released by the doctor.

"If you want to stay, you should. You might even

get a job at the new museum they're opening in town. I hear they still need a curator." He leveled a hard look at her. "You're scared."

Maggie turned away. "Am I? Am I letting fear decide for me?"

A jolt ran down her spine. "Do you think I really could stay? Nathan's Aunt Shirley mentioned a position opening up nearby. That sounds like it would be perfect for me."

He nodded. "I think so, too." Smile lines appeared by his eyes. "And you'll be near Nathan Yazzie."

Heat flooded her face. "Uncle!"

"You think I didn't notice?" His expression was wry. "Everyone noticed."

She buried her face in her hand. "Ugh."

"He's a nice young man. Even if he did try to arrest me."

She looked at him. "He is." The warmth of Nathan's hand on hers, the light of his smile in her hospital room flashed across her mind. "I...I think I want that."

"Then have it. I know I'm not the only one who wants to help you get it."

~

Maggie closed the door to Uncle Thomas's SUV, leaning against its side. She took in the rickety sight of her father's mobile home, backlit by a pink sunset, the mesas casting striking shadows on the horizon. Even the scraggly mesquite tree held a certain charm. It was already starting to feel like home. "So, with a coat of paint and some new furniture, do you think it'd be livable?"

Uncle Thomas circled his SUV and stood before her, the last of the boxes in his arms. "Certainly. I'll even help paint."

She grinned up at him. "You'd really move out here?"

"Yes. For you, I would." He stared at the horizon. "My disagreements with John when I was younger... I felt I needed to get away. But I'm Navajo. This is my home." He looked to her. "It's in my blood, as it is yours."

She nodded and led the way to the front door, holding it open as he carried in her packed boxes.

"Would you like some tea, Uncle?"

He shook his head. "No, I should get back."

She hurried to hug him, and he patted her back. "I'll call you soon, my niece."

Maggie stood at the door, waving until his vehicle was out of sight. She plopped down in the recliner.

"That was Thomas?"

Maggie turned to her mother, who stood by the kitchen in a nightgown and light robe. "Yes. He's pretty great, actually."

"John always spoke of him fondly. To hear your father, his big brother hung the moon."

Maggie grinned. "Yeah. He's not perfect by any means, but he's wise and he cares about people."

"Oh?" Jackie tilted her head, her usually flawless hair a little messy.

"He, um." Maggie took a breath. "He helped me realize some things. Mom, I think I'd like to stay here. I want to move into this mobile home, get a job in Chinle."

Her mother's eyes turned down. "Oh, honey. You have a wonderful job at the University. You love archeology. How could you possibly give that up?"

"I know, and the thought scares me half to death, but I'm going to take a chance. If I move back there, I'll be miserable. I want this family I've discovered here. These wonderful friends." She looked up at her mother's distraught face. "I know it's a huge risk, but I'm going to take the chance."

"Okay. We'll talk about it later."

Maggie nodded. "Okay, Mom. I am pretty tired right now."

Her mother settled in to watch TV, and Maggie clicked the door to the bedroom closed behind her.

She fought the sling to change into her comfiest pajamas and sat on the bed. Her bed. In her home. Her heart was lighter for having made a decision. She looked around her bedroom, her eyes landing on the box of her father's belongings. Maggie reached into it and lifted out the VHS tape. She ran her thumb over it, her nail catching on the subtle grooves. *It's time.*

The TV and a VCR sat on top of the dresser, and Maggie eased the tape inside.

Please, God, please... let my dad be on this video.

Maggie recognized the face that filled the screen from his photos, aged with laugh lines and silver in his hair. Her father looked a lot like Uncle Thomas.

"Margaret."

Tears sprang to her eyes, and Maggie was helpless as they rolled down her cheeks. *My dad's voice.* She wrapped her arm around her middle, holding herself together. Warm, soft, and clear, that was his voice.

"I feel I have little time. If you're watching this,

I'm probably already gone. I tried to reach out to your mother, but she may not have received my letter." A sad smile lifted the corners of his eyes. "This seemed a good plan B.

"I had many things I wanted to say. The most important of these is that I love you. I have loved you since before you were born. I'll love you after the Heavenly Father takes me home. Never, never doubt that. I don't know what's happening in your life now, but I hope you're happy. That you have others who love and care for you. That you're doing work that's meaningful and brings you joy. And that you have your own relationship with God.

"I found the Jesus Road when I was about the age that you are now. His forgiveness changed me, changed the course of my life. Maybe you've heard? John 1:12: 'But as many as received Him, to them He gave the right to become children of God, to those who believe in His name.' If you haven't, please consider it. For me." He paused.

"I have, Dad. You helped me find it."

"There are so many things I never got to tell you. About me, my side of the family. You have a brother, Luke, and my brother Thomas. They can tell you most of it. But you are my daughter." His brows lowered, a determined set to his jaw. "You are Margaret Adakai, of the bilagaàna people, and you were born for the *Kinyaa'áanii*, the Towering House People. Your paternal grandfather is from the Bitter Water clan and your paternal grandmother is of the Sage Brush Hill clan. That is how you are a Navajo woman."

On the screen, her father swallowed heavily. He sighed. "You are my daughter, Margaret. And I am sure, absolutely sure, in my heart, that you'll be a wonderful woman. Know that I am proud of you… will be proud of you." He gave a small smile. "I love you, daughter."

The screen went to static. Maggie wiped her face with her shirtsleeve. *Yes, Dad, I will. I will be the kind of daughter you'd be proud of. I swear it.*

~

Maggie slipped into a plain button-down white shirt, and pulled her dad's silver cross necklace over her head. She lifted the mother of pearl cross to examine it more closely and a warmth spread through her being.

She was ready for this. Ready to visit the little church behind the big fence. Ready to pick up her dad's Bible and start reading it for herself. She knew that somehow, in her heart, she'd already committed herself to this new path on the Jesus Road. Every fiber of her being, told her she was on the right track.

She pulled her mother's car into the gravel parking lot of the church and walked into the building, taking a seat in the very last row. Throughout the church, people gathered into small groups, laughing and chatting before the services started.

Maggie rubbed her hand over her father's Bible. "Lord, please let this be a good day. Please let these people accept me and welcome me as a part of their community."

"Is this seat taken?"

She looked up into Nathan's hesitant face.

~

Nathan pulled the truck through the high chain-link gates and swung it between the faded lines of a parking space. He laid his forehead against the steering wheel.

God, I know I haven't spoken to You much recently. Help me today. Help me in the church, with the congregation, and with whatever I'm gonna say to Maggie.

Because he wasn't sure what he'd say to Maggie, exactly how he was going to approach her. Overhearing half a phone call between Thomas and his mom only told him that she'd be at the church, not how to make her understand what she meant to him. Not how to convince her to stay.

He straightened his posture and his best western-cut shirt. *Time to go.*

He slammed the truck's door behind him, clicking the key fob to lock it with a chirp. He followed the crowd through double doors and into line for a handshake and the weekly bulletin.

After his turn, he stepped to the side of the aisle, letting the overeager air conditioning blast him in the face. He scanned the pews to see a familiar ponytail in the far back corner.

He wrung his flyer between his hands and crossed the room.

"Is this seat taken?"

Maggie's head snapped up from examining a worn black leather Bible, her eyes meeting his. "Nathan?"

He gave a weak smile. "Yeah."

Her eyes went wide, and she scooted to the other side of the bench. "Yes, please, sit." She chuckled. "Somehow, I didn't expect to see you here."

I didn't expect to see me here either. "Yeah. I don't attend that often, but… to be honest, I wanted to see you." He paused. "And I might have come, anyway. Something about you recently has really brought me back to this. You have just kind of modeled how this whole thing," he waved at the room, "is supposed to go."

"I'm glad to see you here."

Nathan nodded. "Yeah, at the least I wanted a chance to say goodbye. But… Maggie, I hope it isn't goodbye. As many times as I warned you off of staying at your dad's mobile home, that threat has passed."

"I know. After a conversation with my uncle, I realized I was afraid, but not of what Luke was doing. I thought I had to have my life planned out. When I stopped to realize I was taking a plunge into the unknown, it freaked me out. All the change, you know." A small smile lit her face. "I guess I'm like my mom in that way. But, unlike her, I'm not letting it stop me." She reached out to him and he took her hand in his—small, warm, but strong. "I'm staying in Chinle."

Nathan let out a breath. "Yeah? So, I'll see you around."

Her fingers curled tighter around his. "You'll be sick of me."

The preacher stepped up to the podium, but Maggie's hand stayed firm in Nathan's. Neither of them let go.

If you liked this book....

You can check out Regina's previous novels, *The Gamble on Love* and *The Long Ride to Love*.

You can follow us and get a free short story at our websites, ReginaRodgers.com and LynLandau.com,
Amazon author pages,
Facebook pages
or Instagrams.

And **please do us the favor of writing a review** for the book on Amazon, Goodreads, and/or Bookbub!